I0620583

# Washington's Salt

Copyright ©, Ray DiZazzo, 2011. All rights reserved.

No part of this book may be printed, used, reproduced or transmitted in any form, or by any means, without written permission of the author, except in cases of brief quotations used in critical articles and reviews.

Published by
Granite-Collen Communications
PO Box 621
Camarillo, CA 93011

This is a work of fiction. All names, characters and incidents are products of the author's imagination. Any resemblance or connection to actual persons, living or dead, events or locations, is strictly coincidental.

Library of Congress Information

Granite-Collen Communications

Printed in the United States of America

ISBN: 0-9648-8002-4
ISBN-13: 9780964880023

# Washington's Salt

Ray DiZazzo

Granite-Collen Communications

# Books by Ray DiZazzo

Clovin's Head

Songs for a Summer Fly

The Car Buyer's Art: How to Beat the Salesman
at His Own Game (with Darrel Parrish)

Corporate Television: A Producer's Handbook

Corporate Scriptwriting: A Professional's Guide

Saying the Right Thing

The Clarity Factor

Corporate Media Production

The Simian Bridge

Moonmare

# Dedication

For Howard, my pal.

# Ceremony

Held still in a wet, moonless night, carpets of jungle lay motionless under the sparkling limbs of Scorpio and Sagittarius. The darkness hummed and snapped with the sounds of exotic insects, and nocturnal creatures called out occasionally from the distant valleys.

Oblivious to these sounds, a group of twelve robed blacks sat in a half circle under the light of a single oil lamp. The lamp hung motionless on a bamboo pole beside the door of a small plywood and sheet metal house in a dirt clearing. Beside the house a muddy pickup truck sat, tailgate down, loaded with cut wood, trowels and carpenter's tools.

A thirteenth black sat at the head of this group facing the others. He led them in a quiet, almost whispered series of chants accompanied by a repetition of slow, swaying movements. Beside the leader a small white terrier, perhaps mesmerized by the rhythmic chanting and swaying, lay with its head on its paws.

Suddenly the door of the house was thrown open and a bone-thin black man burst out, screaming. He wore an oversized red tank top, baggy paisley shorts, and a pair of muddy, untied, Nike Air tennis shoes. A short, chubby woman holding a screaming infant waddled quickly along behind him, pleading hysterically, "Sab ligo! Mon selivoon que sab! Selivoon! Ligo! Ligo!"

The man seemed oblivious to her presence. He ran a few steps straight forward, stopped, his chest heaving, and turned frantically from side to side. Though the group of robed chanters were seated directly to his left, he seemed unaware of their presence. After a short hesitation, he screamed once more and darted toward the treeline. Ahead stood a towering, black wall of vines and leaves, but the man never hesitated. Leaping over a fallen log at a full run, he burst through the foliage and was immediately swallowed by the jungle.

The chubby woman stopped at the log. She knew there were miles of dense vegetation beyond the treeline and getting hopelessly lost in it was as simple as taking a dozen steps then turning around. As the sounds of the man's screams and his body thrashing through vegetation moved farther and farther away, she fell to her knees and continued to scream, "Sab Ligo! Selivoon! Sab! Sab!"

A short time later the chanters got to their feet. The one who led the group pulled the terrier close to his side on a red, rhinestone studded leather leash. With his other hand he made a sign and said quietly, "Quan elisoot sque noon Sab-beot Ligo."

The others nodded, produced flashlights from beneath their robes, and began to walk away single file, down a narrow dirt pathway into the night.

Minutes later, the woman's crying and the screams of her baby were the only sounds that broke the constant inhuman buzz of the jungle night. Finally, far in the distance, the barely discernible screams of a terrified man rang out. The woman held her child tight to her breasts as the sounds slowly died away and then rang out one more time.

A final time...

# One

Norman Miles folded the "Wall Street Journal" in half and placed it on the end table beside his recliner. He yawned briefly, eased his head into the chair's high, tufted pillow back, and closed his eyes.

He felt wonderfully relaxed and peaceful. As he began to slowly drift toward sleep, he became aware of the strong gusts of wind and snow blowing outside. It briefly occurred to him that as long as one was safe, warm, and comfortable in a secure environment, the sounds of harsh weather were not threatening at all. In fact, they created a kind of hypnotic sense of well being…a calling of distant voices…urging him toward sleep.

Moments later Norm's focus shifted to the crackling fire. Now hovering close to unconsciousness, an odd image suddenly sparked in his mind. For a split second he was positive that the crackle of the exploding embers wasn't coming from the fire at all. In that moment, he knew without question that it was actually the sound made by a small boy kneeling on the floor in front of him, smashing the bodies of large, white spiders with a wooden mallet.

As quickly as this image entered his mind, it disappeared. But it had drawn Norm slightly downward, and for several moments he puzzled over it. It wasn't so much that he had imagined it. What perplexed Norm was that it hadn't seemed like a half-dream at all. For that single moment, he was absolutely *positive* that what he was seeing was reality.

The boy was there, kneeling in front of him. He was blond and pale, with a round, freckled face. He was dressed in overalls and a blue and white striped T-shirt, his black and white Vans tennis shoes were covered with mud. He would look up at Norm and smile each time he raised the mallet.

*Each time? Had it happened more than once in the brief instant Norm had seen him? Yes...*

And each time, a spider with a smooth, shiny white body the size of man's fist would crawl slowly out from beneath the recliner between Norm's feet.

The boy's smile would immediately turn to a look of focus and resolve. With a determined scowl, he would lift the mallet over his head, hold it steady, take careful aim, and finally drop the large wooden head directly onto the spider's plump rear end.

Bang!

The shiny white body would burst.

Norm would recoil waiting for the messy result, but amazingly, no guts would splatter. It was as if each of the spiders (*Christ, how many?*) contained only air. They would simply pop like tight, shiny little white balloons, and disappear. One after another. The same look on the boy's face. The same lifting motion. The same brief pause to take aim. Like a piece of film repeating itself over and over...

As Norm pondered this, another sound had begun somewhere close to him. At first, even though it was distinctly audible, he remained unaware of it. In time, though, he did notice it. It was something like a gentle sighing—

the release of a breath with just the slightest hint of vocal texture. The wind? Rushing over the cabin's wooden siding? Carrying circular swirls of snow and blackness into the pines?

No. It was coming from behind Norm. He suddenly became aware of that much. But he cared little about that revelation because in spite of the sounds, his mind was drifting off to another place.

The spiders and the boy had disappeared.

Now, below Norm a parade of larva was moving, "swimming", over a dark, humid landscape overgrown with foliage. Norm was gliding with them, trails of stars over his shoulder, soaring over the soft, glistening white bodies as they passed under waving ferns, moving to the sound of wind...the sound of the sighs.

The sighs. Little by little they seemed to get louder. Insisting...calling....

Eventually Norm's semi-conscious mind had no choice. It began to ponder the sighs. They seemed stronger and less like the wind. They contained more of a vocal quality, coming slowly, one after another, getting slightly louder and more forceful each time.

Suddenly a thought occurred to Norm. He began to realize that what he was hearing sounded like Jane's voice. Stranger still, he noted, was the fact that it had begun to sound like Jane nearing an orgasm! Even in this semi-conscious state, Norm knew that was highly improbable if not virtually impossible. But the sounds persisted. And they got louder. And Norm finally realized they were not like the spiders and larva. They weren't going to drift away into some endless, black monotony of random images. These sounds were…real. *Really* real.

When he came to this realization, Norm was approaching full consciousness.

He opened his eyes.

For several moments he remained perfectly still, his head resting against the back of his recliner. The sounds were indeed being made by Jane. This he knew simply by virtue of the fact that they were the only two people in the cabin on this night. After listening for several seconds and finally making this deduction, he said, "Jane?"

The sighs continued from behind him. In fact, now he noticed they were becoming more like moans and quick husky gasps.

*Impossible*, he thought, now totally conscious.

He leaned forward, wheeled around in his chair and looked back toward the kitchen. During this movement he began to say, "Jane? What the hell is—"

His words were cut off by the sight in front of him.

It *was* Jane.

But something was wrong, very wrong.

She was standing across the room from him in front of the sofa and the end table. She was looking directly at Norm and there were tears in her eyes. The sighs hadn't been sexual at all. She'd been quietly crying. Why, Norm hadn't the slightest idea. But seeing her like this, just standing in the middle of the room staring at him, was somehow frightening. And there was something else. She didn't look exactly like herself. Her face and posture were different somehow. She seemed to be leaning very slightly forward and her eyes looked odd—brighter and more of a pale blue than normal.

Before he could finish his sentence, she sniffed back her tears and wiped her runny nose with the back of her hand. "You know what's wrong, Norm," she said. "Don't sit there and play dumb."

Norm hadn't the slightest idea what she was talking about. "What do you mean?" he said.

"I mean you can play 'Mister Innocent' all you want, but I'm not going to take it…not any more."

"Take what? What the hell are you talking about?"

She paused for a moment, her eyes never leaving his, as if she were carefully thinking over what to say next. Then she took a slow half step toward him. At the same time her head dropped slightly. She seemed to lean farther forward and stare deeper into his eyes. "Norm," she said, her voice rising like a mother about to spank a child if he didn't come clean and admit he'd done something wrong.

When he'd first turned and seen her, Norm had still been slightly disoriented. Now, even though he was fully awake, as she moved slowly toward him his fear deepened. It seemed unthinkable, but she appeared to be making a physically threatening move—like a lioness taking the final few steps before leaping onto her doomed prey. His wife? Crying for some inexplicable reason? Stalking him like a predator?

"Jane!" he said, trembling slightly. "Is this some *joke*?"

Her brilliant eyes seemed to spark on the word "joke."

She stopped her forward movement and again stared for what seemed like a very long time. Then, suddenly, the hint of a smile came to her lips. Not a happy or light smile, but a smile straining to *appear* happy, though seething with a subtext of anger and aggression.

Norm felt his breaths beginning to come more rapidly.

He had no explanation for what was happening or why, but he suddenly felt almost sure he was in danger of some sort of physical attack from his own wife. Again he tried to speak; this time the words almost croaked out. "Jane, for God's sake, will—"

"You don't want to admit it," she snarled, the smile still hovering on her lips. "Fine then. Don't fess up. I'll say it, you...you bastard." She inched closer to him and continued. "You brought me to this. You wouldn't let me stay myself. You made me leave everything I ever wanted...everything, Norm...and become this...this *thing*! My daughter will despise me now. My friends will whisper, 'God!' and turn away. My entire life has been stuffed into a God-damned shit hole because of you!"

"But I don't underst—"

"Do you think I like this?" Her voice was becoming louder as she moved forward. "Do you think hatred and violence look good on me? Do you think I enjoy being bloated and sweaty, with skin like bark? Do you really think my goal in life was to be a putrid fucking conduit for every molecule of sickness in this universe?"

Norm began to hyperventilate. He was trembling violently. "But, Jesus," he blurted out, "I didn't do *anything*!"

She was nearly at his feet. She stopped. She knelt down in front of him and looked up. Suddenly, he could see her face much better in the light of the lamp beside him. Though it was his wife's face, it was slightly rounder, and her skin looked coarse, dried, and pock-marked. She smiled again, now broadly. Her teeth were yellowed and uneven. Her pale blue eyes had become strange, brilliant lights, boring into Norm's soul.

"You opened your eyes, Norm. You killed the spiders. You drew me out of my own sweet skin into this rotting carcass, and you fed my mind to the demons. Now, mother fucker,...you *pay!*"

As she said these words, she reached up and grasped his arm. Her fingers were frigid and hard. The sensation was like nothing Norm had experienced in his life. Her flesh was radiating some icy, evil power, and simply by touching him, she was pouring that evil into Norm. He felt it flowing into his body and mind. His flesh began to rot. His mind became a black sponge, absorbing sickening thoughts and feelings. His bones ached. His eyes began to swell and bleed. He was becoming a demon.

He screamed.

All traces of Norman Miles was sucked from his body in one frigid, unholy blast.

He fell forward into the darkness.

⚑

"Norm! Norman, my God!"

It was Jane's voice ringing in the blackness. "Sweetheart!"

The light began to seep back in, carrying a sickening wave of horror along with the memory of what he had just experienced.

Norm opened his eyes. He was on the floor.

Jane was kneeling over him, saying, "Honey, what happened?" She was trembling and looked frightened out of her wits, but she was herself—the real Jane. His wife. *Really* her.

In the first instant after he'd opened his eyes, this realization filled Norm with an incredible sense of relief. His wife was okay. She was not angry...not evil.

Immediately following this, however, the wave of horror flooded back in. What he had just seen was *real*! There was no question. Like any normal person, he had experienced dreams all his life. Even the most vivid and frightening nightmares couldn't begin to compare with the reality of the images he had just witnessed. It had happened—*really happened*!

But somehow the real Jane was back.

She broke into his fear and confusion. "Honey, my God! Did you fall? What's the matter, for God's sake!"

Norm was now getting a hold on himself. He got to his knees and looked around. Again, the wave of horror. It *couldn't* be. He'd *seen* her.

"Norman, speak to me!" She shook him. "Norman! Norman!"

"Jesus!" he finally breathed.

"Honey, what happened?"

"I...Jane, I...It was *real*!"

"What?"

"You...You were back there. By the sofa. You came forward, and...God!"

"It was a dream, Norm."

"No."

"I was in the kitchen getting our cocoa. Look." She gestured to two mugs of cocoa sitting on the end table beside the recliner.

"No, Jane. You were there. I swear!"

"But honey, I *wasn't*! You had some sort of nightmare."

"No! Honest to God, your face was…Jesus, grotesque and you—"

"Norman, my God!" Jane could see her husband was becoming hysterical. She shook him. Sternly, she snapped, "Norman! Listen to me! I'm here. It's *me*. I am perfectly fine. You had a *dream*! A very bad, very vivid *dream*!"

It worked. He began to believe her. Jane wouldn't allow him to slip back. She tugged on him saying, "Get up. Here, get into your chair."

Still dazed and only partially oriented, he followed her instructions. She handed him one of the mugs saying "Here. Take a sip."

He sipped. It tasted warm and comforting. Real.

Jane could see he was beginning to come around. She thought about calling Urgent Care, but decided to wait. It was 9:30 p.m., snow was blowing outside, and the Urgent Care facility was an hour's drive down the mountain in Pomona. Though the trip down was one she didn't relish the thought of making, she'd decided that if he didn't come around in the next few minutes, she would call ahead, then put him in the car and go.

Placing the mug of cocoa aside, he looked at her and smiled weakly. "You're right," he said. "It was a dream. But Christ, what a dream…"

He opened his arms and she fell into them.

# TWO

Kelly Miles pulled her black Dodge Stealth up in front of the Alpha Cigna fraternity house and left the engine running. She checked her watch. 5:00 p.m. She tooted the horn. When no response came after nearly a minute, she tooted again, this time "leaning" on it for good measure. Still, no response. 5:02.

She turned off the ignition, got out of the car, and walked up the cracked sidewalk overgrown with weeds to a brown, paint-chipped front door. She banged the door-knocker several times. No answer. She knocked loudly and shouted, "Eric!" Nothing. She repeated herself, this time yelling louder. Finally she heard movement inside.

A few seconds later, the door opened. It was dark inside. The stale, sickening, yeasty smell of day old beer, smoke, and dirty socks drifted into Kelly's face. Eric Harmon stepped out into the brilliant afternoon sun in his red satin boxer shorts. His thick blond hair was matted and mussed and the whites of his almond eyes were saturated with red. "Fuck!" he said, as his face met the bright orange sunlight. "What time is it?"

Kelly shook her head and said, "God!"

Eric just may have been the most attractive male student at Chico College. His thin, calendar good looks made him stand out immediately in a crowd and drew females like moths, which, of course, was part of his and Kelly's problem. But not the main part. Since he and Kelly had become an exclusive thing she hadn't worried so much about whether he had been true to her. She felt Eric cared very much for her, and she believed him when he said he had remained hers alone. But that didn't stop the "action" from coming his way, and he was weak when it came to parties. Though he was a great guy at heart, he tended to want to be the life of the party—every party. That meant too much drinking and all night, all day ragers, which Kelly knew was his problem at this moment.

Of more concern to her was the fact that Eric had also recently begun using cocaine. A week earlier, when they'd been making love, he had actually tried to get her to snort it at the last moment. She'd refused and that had led to a major fight. In the end she'd given in to him, as she typically did, and tried it that one time. It had done absolutely nothing for her and, in fact, ruined the sex altogether. But because she'd given in, he'd promised he'd quit using it himself and slow down on his drinking as well. So, the cocaine he'd stopped, but obviously the drinking was another story. "It's five! We've got to go! You were supposed to be ready!"

He looked around rubbing his eyes with both palms. "Jesus, I don't know, Kel," he said.

"No way! Come on, Eric. You *promised*! And they're waiting to meet you."

"How long is it?"

"Seven hours. But I said I'd drive. Now come on!"

"God, seven fucking hours! Man, that's bizarre!"

"It's all planned, Eric. And you knew that and promised! You can sleep all the way up!"

After more stammering and huffing, Eric finally gave in. "Shit. Okay, damn it. Hang on." And with that he turned and stepped back into the frat house.

Kelly followed. One sleeping form lay spread on the couch partially wrapped in a blanket. Another was curled up in front of the TV. A third was stretched out on the breakfast bar bordering the kitchen. Beer and wine bottles and full ashtrays sat on nearly every piece of furniture. The house stunk like a brewery and Kelly now noticed that the stale odor was mixed with the strong, lingering smell of perfume. She felt the urge to gag, and brought her hand up to her mouth.

Following Eric to his room, she stepped in and saw a thin, curled up figure wrapped in a sheet on his bed, topped by a mane of long blond hair. Before she had a chance to say a word, Eric threw his hands up and said, "Relax, she's Mark's. I caught a few winks in the den."

Kelly glared at him as he removed his shorts, wrapped a towel around his thin tanned body, and started toward the shower.

# Three

Professor Carl Maddy kneeled in the "Quarterly-Scholarly" section of the Pierson College Library and quickly shoved several piles of back issues of "New Chemist" onto the carpeted floor. The instant each stack hit, he began picking up the small quarterlies individually, and rapidly leafing through each Table of Contents.

The first dozen did not produce what he was searching for. As he finished with each, he slung it to the side and quickly reached for the next one. Three more issues and he still hadn't found what he was after. "Damn!" he said out loud, "I know you're here, man. Come on!"

Five more issues. Nothing.

Then, finally, he had it. "New Chemist Quarterly, Volume VII, January/March, 2004".

The title he'd been after read: "Rare Substances of the Western Caribbean: A Cataloging and Overview", by Martin Sellis, Ph.D., Farinel University.

"Sellis!" Maddy exclaimed, finally remembering the name. "Of course!"

He flipped to page seventeen and began scanning the article. It was a long piece, running nearly twenty pages, but it didn't take Maddy long to find the two words he was after. Once he did, he began to read quickly, and soon confirmed what he had been afraid of most of this evening.

With the magazine in hand, he got to his feet. He rushed out of the library and into the elevator. Moments later, he exited three floors down and quickly made his way through several hallways. Finally, he unlocked a large white door and stepped into the chemistry lab on the first floor of Building C.

He rushed past the groups of microscopes, sinks, and Bunsen burners. A door marked "Lab Office" stood ajar beside a tall, metal wall rack containing test tubes, beakers, plastic jugs and a variety of aluminum tools. He hurried into the office, took a seat at the cluttered desk and looked at his watch. 9:10 p.m.

He picked up the phone. "Sorry, Avery," he said to himself and dialed.

Seven miles away, Professor Avery McCall was lying on his bed, watching the channel five evening news. His wife, Joan, was snuggled up on her side of the bed, snoring lightly.

The top local stories had just been reported and anchor Bonnie Mulette was beginning "News From Around the World". As footage of yet another international crisis began to play, McCall yawned and moved his finger to the "Power" button on the remote control.

Suddenly the phone rang.

The Professor jumped. His wife continued to snore, never missing a beat. McCall picked up the phone immediately and answered, "Hello."

"Avery, this is Carl," Maddy said quickly.

"Carl. What's the matter?"

"I've got a weird problem. I need a phone number."

"Where are you?"

"At the lab."

McCall shook his head. "Don't you ever go home, Carl?"

"I'll take the lecture tomorrow," Maddy said. "Right now can you please help me locate a guy?"

"Who?"

"Think back about four years. We had a seminar. I think they called it "Future Directions?"

"Right. I remember."

"There was a panel brought in by Johnson, and one guy was a specialist on rare substances." Carl looked at the magazine in front of him as he continued. "Martin Sellis."

"Right. From Farinel. Hell of a background. He'd been running around in the Caribbean or something."

"Exactly. Well, I need his phone number."

"Now?"

"This minute."

"What's going on?"

"Look, Avery, I don't have time now. I know you'll have him in that all inclusive "who's who" of yours and I need to call him right away."

"Christ, Carl, can't it-"

"Avery, this is important. It's critical. Please?"

"Hang on." Avery reached for the nightstand and found his glasses. He then rolled his plump figure out of bed with a hefty groan, pushed the hold button on the phone, and hung it up. His wife continued to snore. He threw on his robe and waddled out of his bedroom. He made his way down the hall into his study and turned on his desk light. There, he removed the book Maddy had referred to from a drawer and began to look up Sellis. As he did this, he picked up the desk phone. "You still there?"

"Yeah."

"Okay, just a minute…Here we go. Sellis, Martin Sellis. Ready?"

"Shoot."

"(415) 555-1567. Now, that was a few years ago. I don't—"

"Thanks, Avery. Talk to you Monday."

Avery heard the line click at the other end. He paused for a second, then shook his head. As he hung up the phone and moved back to his bed, he thought to himself that aside from the urgent request for the phone number, Carl was acting pretty much as he always did. With no kids, very few close friends, and an insatiable passion for molecular exploration, his life was essentially contained between the four walls of the college lab. He taught five days a week and often spent weekends and evenings there with his eye to a microscope.

As Avery slid between the covers and turned off the TV, he was curious, however. Why Sellis's phone number? And why at this time of the night? No problem, he finally decided as he pulled up the covers, nudged his wife to stop her from snoring, and rolled onto his side. He'd find out soon enough.

When Carl Maddy hung up on Avery, he didn't hesitate for a second. With the phone number and Sellis's article in hand, he immediately began to dial.

# Four

Norm and Jane had finished two cups of cocoa each and re-stoked the fire before concluding that Norm had simply had a vivid and bizarre nightmare.

Before reaching that conclusion, they had talked at length about other possibilities. Could there have been some problem with the dinner she had fixed earlier? Where and when had they gotten the ingredients? Had any packages been open on the shelf from prior use?

When these turned up no plausible explanation for what had happened, the couple settled on the nightmare theory and agreed not to let a freak incident ruin this first evening of their holiday in the mountains.

Though Jane didn't say so, one other possibility did secretly concern her. She knew that Norm had been under unusual pressure lately, and it was just a few days ago that he had mentioned he'd been having trouble sleeping. Though he seemed to be himself and fully recovered from this evening's incident, Jane couldn't get the image out of her mind of how convinced he had been that what he'd seen was real. Because of this, the fear of some sort of impending breakdown hovered in the back of her mind. She suspected, and was right in assuming, that Norm harbored the same unspoken fear about himself.

To stay off the subject, however, both he and Jane had turned the conversation to the one person in their lives just as important as each other—Kelly.

"When is she due in?" Norm asked.

"She said around midnight."

Norm looked at the cabin window. The gusts of snow were howling in the pines. "She have chains?" he asked.

"A brand new set," Jane replied. "There was a sale at Olson's. I told her to put a set on the credit card before she left. She refused."

"To buy them?"

"To put them on the card. You think they'll come up?"

"I'll bet they'll stay down below at The Kingston, and come up in the morning."

Jane smiled. "Our daughter?"

Norm returned the smile. "Tell me about this new guy."

"Eric's his name. He's a PE major, and she says he's God's gift to the feminine species."

Norm shook his head. "Here we go again. What is this, the third guy in the past year?"

"She just turned twenty-one, Norm. She's supposed to be playing the field."

"Playing the field is fine, but it seems like every guy we hear about is 'the one' and it turns out they're all a bunch of lunch-heads. PE major, for Christ sakes."

"He's planning on teaching, I guess."

"Oh, now there's a lucrative endeavor."

"All I know is our daughter is head-over-heels for the guy and we're going to be nice to him...right?"

Norm shook his head again. Begrudgingly he said, "Are we ever anything else?" He had reason to be cynical. Norm and Jane both knew their daughter was a very bright and independent young woman in many ways. She was punctual, neat, a near perfect student and, since she'd turned sixteen, she'd always insisted on working, keeping a checking account of her own, and paying her own way. When it came time to send her to college, Norm and Jane had had to work very hard to get her to agree that they would pay and her savings would remain invested.

In the opposite sex department, however, she was a different person. She was insecure, anxious, and it seemed to Norm and Jane, acutely worried at the "ripe old" age of twenty-one that if she didn't snatch the right guy soon, she'd end up a spinster. He and Jane had pondered the question of how she could be so different when it came to her love life. The only possible reason they could think of was that Kelly had always been overweight. As hard as she'd tried over the years, she'd never quite been able to drop and keep off the roughly twenty-five pounds that took her out of the "thin" category and labeled her that dreaded word—"plump."

"We've never been anything else but nice to her boy-friends," Jane responded, "and that's exactly the way it should be. I just wish they'd get here so we can stop worrying."

"So give her a call."

Jane thought about it. "Why not," she said, moving to a telephone on the end table beside the sofa. She dialed. Moments later Kelly answered. "Hi Honey. Where are you?"

When the call came in, Kelly had just finished filling her gas tank. "Hi Mom," she said, sliding into the driver's seat and reaching for her seatbelt. "We're in Van Nuys. Just gassed up."

"How's Eric doing? Is he helping you drive?"

She looked to her right. Eric was just stepping out of the gas station mini-mart after a bathroom visit. He had a bounce in his step and a smile on his face. "He's fine. Just finished his latest pit stop. He'll drive if I ask."

"Is it raining there?"

"Yeah, but not real hard."

"It's coming down up here."

"Rain?"

"Snow. And it's really howling."

"Great! If it blows through tonight, the lift will be in full swing tomorrow!"

"You brought your chains, right?"

"You know I did."

"Good. Be safe. If the road is closed or you don't feel like coming up tonight, just stay down below at the Inn and come up in the morning."

"We'll be fine, Mom. Don't wait up."

"Okay, you take care. Dad sends his love."

"See you soon."

Jane hung up. "Everything good?" Norm asked.

"Fine."

"She knows this road like the back of her hand. And we both know she's too damn sensible to risk trouble." As he said this, Norm checked his watch. 9:22 p.m. "You getting tired?" he asked.

"A little," Jane responded feeling a knot begin to tighten in her stomach.

"Well, I'm not crazy about the idea of going back to sleep just yet, but why don't we relax on the bed and watch some TV. Maybe we'll both eventually just drift off."

"Sounds cozy," Jane answered, forcing a smile.

Twenty minutes later they were watching a documentary on Spain on the Discovery Channel. Norm was in his pajamas sitting against the headboard with his pillow tucked into the small of his back. He was still anxious about going to sleep himself, and hoped Jane would stay awake longer, maybe to talk some more.

That was not to be the case, however. Roughly ten minutes after they had turned on the TV, Jane took off her glasses and placed them on the nightstand beside her. She rolled part way over and said "Honey, I'm not going to last."

Norm felt a twinge of anxiety in his stomach as he answered, "Sack out. I'll be up for a few more minutes."

"You feel okay, now?"

"I'm fine."

"You sure?"

"Positive."

With that he turned and kissed her. She rolled over, bunched up her pillow and became quiet.

Norm looked at the clock on his nightstand. 9:46 p.m.

The wind continued to howl.

⚒

Jane had no idea how long she'd slept, nor did she realize it at first when something began drawing her toward consciousness.

It began in her dream with the movement of a pickup truck. The truck had hitched up to a small, silver Airstream trailer she was sleeping in. She hadn't seen it hook up, but she knew it had, and she knew it was a pickup. Then it began to move, pulling the trailer forward out of a sun blazed, grassy spot in a small trailer park somewhere in the South…pulling it over bumpy, dirt roads.

As the wheels rolled from rut to rut, the trailer swayed slightly back and forth. This comforting motion rocked Jane gently in her sleep. Somewhere in her mind she thought to herself, what a peaceful feeling—as if she'd returned to infancy and was on some wonderful cross-country road trip with her parents.

Soon she began to realize that as soothing as the motion might seem, it was pulling her farther and farther upward, out of sleep, toward a bedroom in a snowstorm. This she didn't like. Not because she disliked the bedroom or was concerned about the storm. It was just that the tranquil motion was so peaceful, so comforting…

Moments later, as she came close to consciousness, the movement changed. She noticed that it had become less rhythmic and predictable. Instead of a repetitive motion, it had turned to a kind of random, slight, jerking movement. Soon after this, she became aware that it was indeed a movement of her bed, but a truck was not pulling her and she was not in a trailer. She was lying in the bedroom of their mountain cabin.

And her bed was moving…

The movement stopped for a long moment, then it came again, gently.

In the cabin. With Norm.

*Norm*!

She drew a breath and opened her eyes. Her head was still buried in the pillow. Directly in front of her face was the telephone and the digital clock face. The glowing green display numbers read 11:07 p.m.

The movement came again.

She swung around and upward to a sitting position.

Norm was leaning, almost half-sitting against her side of the bed near the footboard. He was wearing his pajamas and facing toward the wall. His head was bowed as if he were sad or depressed. Though the room was dark and she couldn't quite make out the details of his profile, Jane could tell there was some subtle difference in the way he looked.

At the moment, however, this was the least of her worries. Waking out of a dead sleep and turning to find him sitting there had shocked her. She found herself trembling, having difficulty speaking as she forced out, "N...Norm—?"

He cut her off. "Hi," he said quietly, without ever lifting his head or facing her. His voice was different, too. It was Norm, but there was something odd in the tone or voice quality of his words. They seemed deeper and rolled out of his mouth with a subtle drawl.

She paused, waiting for him to continue, and realized that her hand, resting on her right leg, was shaking. When he said nothing more, she tried again. In a quavering voice, she said. "Wha...what are you doing, Hon?"

"You fucked things up," he said very quietly and matter-of-factly.

Her eyes were adjusting. She was beginning to make out detail in the darkness. Though he was still facing away, she could see his face a little better. Something was...

Her trembling increased. Her breath seemed to be leaving her. "But...I don't—"

"You and old Doppy," he said, again, cutting her off.

Doppler? Their Irish Setter? He'd died two years earlier!

"Bastard wouldn't stay down, Jane. You just couldn't let him go, could you?"

Nearly croaking with fear, Jane whispered, "But Doppy's been dead for—"

At that moment, Norm lifted his head, turned toward her and smiled. His face suddenly became visible in the dim green glow of the clock display.

By reflex alone, Jane jumped and gasped, "*God!*"

What she saw was, and was, *not* her husband.

It was Norm's face, but oddly different. His nose seemed slightly enlarged and lower on his face. His skin looked overly tanned and hardened. His eyes were much brighter than normal. They were slightly askew in the sockets and sunk deeper into his leathery face. And his lips. They were large, pale, smiling casually at her.

The instant they faced each other Jane knew something was horribly wrong. Though this appeared to be her husband, she was staring into the face of someone or something else. Something evil. And who or whatever it was, it was sitting at the foot of her bed smiling at her.

In a quiet, casual tone he continued on the subject of Doppler. "That old fuck? Dead? No way."

Jane remained still, trembling, saying nothing.

"Probably my fault," he said. And now he was smiling broadly, exposing large white teeth. His brilliant eyes had become beacons, spotlights.

"Right?" he asked.

She remained silent.

Suddenly, his tone became almost playful. "But hey!" he chuckled, "I brought old Doppy home!"

Jane felt her chest constrict. The evil intensified. She whined under her breath.

"Maybe you could fix him up. See he's…well, he's not feeling real great." With this, he got to his feet. For a long horrifying moment, he seemed to lean forward and stare deep into Jane's soul with those bright blue eyes. Trying to burn his way in…take control. Then, suddenly, his stare released her. He turned and moved around to the foot of the bed. He reached toward the floor saying, "Not much waggin' goin' on these days for the old bastard."

Jane heard clinking. A chain? A dog tag? Something heavy was beginning to move. A horrible odor wafted towards her.

Norm stepped back around to the side of the bed in full view of Jane. He was smiling broadly and holding up the limp, dripping body of her beloved Irish Setter.

At first Jane thought it was the dog's dug up carcass. It was covered in mud and dirt and smelled musty and fetid. Then, suddenly, she saw something. A slight movement. The shoulder flinched. A muscle had moved. This was followed by a slight, high-pitched whine.

Jane tried to scream. She couldn't. She tried to get to her feet and run, but couldn't move. She realized the demon had won. She felt all sanity and goodness drawn from her body in a long, sickening vacuum.

As her Irish Setter suddenly cried out in pain, she was pulled toward him into hot, humid blackness…

⋈

"Jane! Jane!" He was shaking her, calling, pulling her back.

Norman. He was above her, kneeling over her on the bed. For an instant she was confused, wondering what had just happened. Then, like a ghastly flood of repulsion, it swept over her. *Norm*! *Doppy*! She lurched upward, gasping, looking toward the foot of the bed.

No Doppy.

"Honey!" Norm shouted, as if he, too, was scared out of his wits. "What is it? *Sweetheart*!"

Jane began to gather her wits. She was with Norm... the *real* Norm! She was okay. It had been a...*No*, she thought, it couldn't possibly have been a dream! He had *been* there. She had *seen* him, heard him, and smelled the warm sickening coat of her dead dog.

"Jane! Are you okay?" Norm shouted, shaking her more firmly.

"My God, N...Norm," she managed to gasp.

"What was it?"

"Y...you! You were...Oh, God, *Doppy*!" She began to tremble and cry hysterically. Norm could see she was losing control. He pulled her tightly into his arms, squeezed her to his body, comforting her, saying, "It's okay, honey. It was a dream! It never really happened."

As he said this, Norm stared across the room at the gusts of snow howling past the window. He wondered what in God's name was happening to he and his wife.

# Five

Martin Lanteon was a black man of commanding presence. His slender, six foot four inch frame, British Caribbean accent, and typically impeccable dress helped draw the immediate attention, and often admiration, of the people he met. And once Lanteon had their attention, he was a master at completing the image of himself as a charming, influential and very wealthy man.

People who knew Lanteon only briefly, or on an infrequent basis, sometimes kept this opinion of him. Those who knew him more intimately, however, such as his employees and close business associates, came to realize quickly that he was a very selfish, often angry, and potentially violent individual.

On this day, however, Lanteon was smiling.

He'd just made a visit to the mountains. He'd driven a pot-holed, two lane road out of the city of Georgetown, Grand Cayman, climbing over a thousand feet to the sparsely populated village of Venon Loquel. Little more than a bus stop with a few stores and barns and lots of chickens, the village also had a tiny Post Office annex and several clusters of shacks and hovels half buried in jungle foliage.

Villages like this were common on the island of Grand Cayman, but they weren't Lanteon's typical haunts. Today was different. He had come to spend time with an old woman and her thirteen-year-old granddaughter—both of whom knew the brutal side of Lanteon. Their true feelings for him remained hidden, however, because he had come with something special for them—one hundred dollars.

The old woman and the child smiled and bowed repeatedly as Lanteon removed the individual ten dollar bills slowly from his wallet and placed them on a small wicker table under a canopy of huge ferns and palm trees. A hundred dollars would go a very long way in a remote place like Venon Loquel.

Prior to handing over the money, Lanteon had spent a good bit of time with the two women. He'd insisted on being present while they provided an important service to him. After a brief discussion, he simply took a seat in their quaint living room and waited patiently as the events he had come to witness transpired. Later, satisfied they had done their job well, Lanteon smiled broadly and thanked them as he peeled off the bills. And this time his smile was sincere. He felt a great sense of self-satisfaction and retribution, knowing that a wrong had been made right.

He bid good day to the women and left their shaded backyard. He walked around the side of their small house, then down a short, overgrown dirt path that led to a rotting wooden bridge. He crossed the bridge, passed several more houses half submerged in ferns and palms, and came to a "T" in the path. He turned right, walked nearly a hundred yards, and finally emerged from the lush green canopy only a few yards from his gold Mercedes Benz. It was parked in the shade under a cluster of banana trees beside the bus stop.

Three locals were seated in the sticky, blistering sunlight waiting for the bus. Two played a board game with a round stone and pegs. The third sat on a gas can, smiling at Lanteon as he approached.

Lanteon nodded and smiled back.

"G'day," the smiling man said in a gravely Caribbean voice.

"An' you," Lanteon responded. He then hopped into his car and immediately turned on the ignition and the air conditioner. He pulled away off the gravel area and made his way along a one-lane dirt road for nearly a mile. At a fork in the road he turned left, and in a few minutes was back on the pot-holed, two-lane road leading down the mountain.

He checked his watch. 12:00 p.m. He would be back in Georgetown easily by 1:00 p.m. Just in time for his meeting with the Vice President of the London Bank.

# Six

By 10:50 p.m. Kelly and Eric had nearly reached Mountain Avenue in Pomona. With the exception of their recent gas stop, a fast food drive-in, and several bathroom stops for Eric, they had come straight through. On the north side of the city, Mountain Avenue turned into Highway 18. This became the access road through the small mountain communities of Running Springs and Blue Jay that ultimately led to the Mount Baldy Resort area and the Miles' cabin.

The couple had been moving through a steadily increasing rain since just after leaving the gas station. Kelly had noticed that Eric had become quiet and distant. He had seemed to become almost spooked as the time passed and the rain intensified.

"You sure you know where the hell you're going?" he asked finally, peering though the sweeping windshield wipers.

Kelly had been cautious because of the rain and low visibility, but she wasn't spooked at all. Her parents had owned the cabin at Baldy since shortly after the sale of their first travel book, some nine years ago. At that time, Kelly had been a pigtailed, twelve-year-old. A least a half dozen times a year she'd ridden up from their Studio City home in the back of the family SUV surrounded by friends, board games, blankets, and pillows. She'd often recalled how those had been some of the happiest times of what she considered a nearly a perfect childhood.

Four years later, she began driving up to the cabin herself, usually with the same group of girlfriends. They would ski in the winter, sun themselves in the summer at the nearby resort on Lake Gregory, and generally have a ball—most times as a treat from Norm and Jane. Because of these trips, Kelly knew exactly where she was, and had no worries that they would reach the cabin safely. She did have one concern, however, and that was *when* they would reach it. She knew that at this time of the year the snow often meant road closures, chains, and generally danger-ous driving conditions. "We're almost to Pomona," she said reassuringly. "Mountain Avenue is about ten miles ahead. It takes us straight up the mountain. You ever put chains on a car?"

This seemed to spook Eric even worse. *"Chains*? Hell, no. Why?"

"It's snowing up top," Kelly said. "The road'll probably be icy."

"Great!" Eric pouted. "Nice fucking move, Kelly."

Kelly could see his anxiety was getting worse. "God, relax!" she said. "It's not a problem. We'll check in with my folks on the weather."

"Right. And suppose they say it's a freakin' blizzard up there?"

"Then we put on the chains, and go slow!"

"How far is it up the mountain?"

"It takes about an hour."

"And it's safe in this kind of weather?"

"Yes. You just have to be careful."

"Shit," Eric said, shaking his head and wishing he'd never agreed to go on this trip. He knew of at least two "ragers" going on over the holiday weekend back in Chico. Both would be jamming at this minute. There would be plenty of beer, shooters and rocks, not to mention at least one choice piece of ass at each party—*if* he was able to ditch Kelly, that is.

As he thought about that possibility, it occurred to him that it was just about time to dump this chunky, spoiled little bitch with the rich parents and the moral code of a nun. She had been an excellent lay, he conceded to himself, and she'd actually been different and fun for a while. He had to admit to himself that at first, even though she was a little porky, he'd been genuinely attracted to her. She was intelligent and he'd enjoyed her company and conversation. But lately, she'd been getting on his nerves. The intelligent conversation had become more and more like a series of lectures, continually focusing on how Eric should dump his bad habits, and, though she never really said it, "grow up". Conversation was fine. Lectures Eric could do without. On top of this, there were plenty of other good lays around for the taking. And though most of them probably wouldn't have anything intelligent to say, they were thinner, hotter looking, and probably great fucks. He also knew of a few who would share a snort with him and get off on a little kink between the sheets.

At this point he knew he had no choice but to finish this idiotic trip, but that, he decided, would be it. When he got back, Kelly was history. And the first babe he planned to call was Myrna, the one he had nailed earlier that day at the frat party.

"God," Kelly said. "How come you're so *upset*? I mean, so it's snowing. That's cool. The lift'll be open and we can ski for free. My dad has an annual pass. I thought that's what we wanted?"

"If we ever get there," Eric said sarcastically.

"Look," Kelly said, "if it's really bad, we'll get a room tonight down below and go up first thing in the morning."

"Where?"

"There's a little motel right at the base of the mountain."

"Fine," Eric said, still staring out at the howling darkness that surrounded them.

Kelly knew Eric was pissed, but she was surprised to sense the fear in him. He almost seemed like a small boy afraid of having the light turned off in his bedroom. And there was something else that bothered her. He seemed more than just mad or frightened. Over just the last hour, he had seemed to actually become agitated and sarcastic. While she'd seen him mad before, and on occasion even callous and insensitive, this tone was new.

As she moved forward through the night, with silence between her and this boy she cared so much for, she told herself it was just the darkness and the weather. Maybe as a small boy he'd had some traumatic experience in a bad storm, or at night. Whatever it was, she told herself *not* to start getting insecure about her body. *He cares,* she said to herself. *He said so. And he's mine. The sexiest guy in Chico, and he's all mine——- chubby or not.* She continued these mental pep talks for the next ten miles, but a seed had been planted. The insecurity she could never quite shake, was growing in her again.

Ten minutes later, when she pulled into the strip mall beside The Kingston Inn, Eric was still pouting, staring into the night.

# Seven

Before he finished dialing, Professor Carl Maddy suddenly decided to hang up.

It occurred to him that before he called a man with the stature of Doctor Martin Sellis, he should be as scientifically prepared as possible. Then, when he reached Sellis, rather than come off as some bumbling weekend warrior, he would present himself as a competent chemistry professor with what could well be a very important discovery. This meant he had to go back over the tests he had done on the substance in the lab earlier, and briefly document what his results had been.

He returned to the lab, and with pen and paper in hand, began to recall and note the evening's events. He'd begun, simply enough, with a low magnification, visual examination under the microscope. He'd noted that the substance seemed almost pure white with a wrinkled, almost rubbery outer texture. This finding immediately eliminated the possibility of it being a crystal, even though he had never come across a pure white, non-crystalline in all his years in chemistry.

After his initial visual examination, he'd started working with a very fine pick to tear a flake of the substance open. Though this should have been simple enough, it had taken some doing because the rubbery, almost slippery consistency of the material made it difficult to hold down and rip. Eventually, with the use of a pair of micro tweezers and a pick, he was able to make the tear. At that point, the inside cross section of the flake became visible, and this offered yet another surprise. The flake seemed to be made up of rows of extremely tiny white sacks. After boosting the magnification considerably and pulling the cross section farther open, he verified this was true. The sacks were like clusters of microscopic white grapes attached along veins lined up in perfectly neat symmetrical rows.

At that point, he'd gotten a much finer pick and poked a hole in one of the sacks. Still another surprise. Nothing happened—- at first. After he'd put considerable pressure on the sack with the side of his pick, a thick, lumpy, greenish jelly oozed out very slowly. As it erupted up through the hole in the sack, it occurred to Maddy that it looked very much like green cottage cheese in a clear fatty gel.

Never in all his years had he viewed a substance at the near cellular level and seen anything like this. It was then that he began to feel that he'd gotten his hands, not only on something odd, but some sort of extremely rare substance.

Next he'd exposed the substance to water and found absolutely no permeation or dilution at all. It was like trying to mix a sealed, oily glob in a clear plastic pouch with a micro drop of water. The two remained separate entities, even when Maddy had tried to force the water into the substance by poking it with holes and surrounding it with a droplet.

Temperature and pressure tests came next. And again the results were strange. At extremely low temperatures the liquid appeared to freeze solid, as he would have expected. But at increased temperatures, those only slightly above normal for the human body, the substance began taking on an orange hue. As Maddy increased both the temperature and began to add pressure, it turned to a brilliant orange and almost seemed to begin glowing! When this happened, Maddy made a quick reflexive adjustment to drop the temperature immediately and to his amazement, the specimen suddenly *vaporized*—not slowly as if it were evaporating, or even quickly. Rather, it happened in an instant! As if some invisible, incredibly powerful force had instantaneously blown it into oblivion!

When Carl had seen this, he'd pulled back from the lens and spoken out loud to himself, something he actually did quite often when he was alone. "What the fuck?" he'd said at first. "No way, man!" He'd then taken a second look, repeated the procedure with a new sample of the substance and gotten the same result. "Carl, old boy," he'd finally concluded, "I don't know what the hell you got here, buddy but this I *can* tell you. It ain't fuckin' salt."

A series of exposure tests had followed, using organic elements—minerals, plant cells, and various proteins. It was the last of these exposure tests that had cinched his earlier hunch—that this was not just an odd substance, but also something very dangerous he'd once heard or read about. This, in turn, had prompted his search through the old periodicals, and eventually his call to Avery.

Now, with the telephone number of Martin Sellis in hand, and scribbled notes laid out in front of him, he dialed again.

Moments later, it was answered. "Hello," Maddy said, "Doctor Sellis?"

"Yes," came the answer.

"Doctor Martin Sellis?"

"Yes."

"Doctor Sellis, my name is Carl Maddy. I teach chemistry at Pierson College. I believe I'm in possession of some Kaseentilineol Hydrophoxine."

When Sellis heard this, he immediately sat straight up in bed and reached for his glasses.

# Eight

After Jane's episode, it had taken Norm a good ten minutes to calm his wife down completely. When he'd accomplished this, both he and Jane decided that since sleep seemed to be required to bring on the terrible nightmare's they'd experienced, they would both simply have to stay awake all night, until whatever it was had worn off.

They'd then moved to the kitchen, made a pot of coffee, and begun discussing what could possibly be causing the dreams.

"It's got to be some sort of drug," Norm said. "What else could do that?"

"But a drug that only takes effect when you sleep?" Jane questioned.

It seemed odd, Norm agreed, but he had no better explanation. Then, after a moment, he added to her theory saying, "Maybe it only takes affect at a certain level of consciousness, or when the respiration slows, or hell, I don't know. It could be anything. That's the point. We have no idea."

"What about the 'Salt'?", Jane asked.

Norm thought about this. In one way it made sense. It was the only different thing he could remember that they had ingested in the past few weeks, but that also made a pretty solid argument against it. "We've been eating it for weeks. How many times? A half a dozen?"

Jane thought back. "Probably," she said.

"So why now, all of a sudden?"

"I don't know. Maybe it builds up in the system?"

"Could be. But I do know this. If Carl's had any chance at all to look at the stuff, he's probably done it by now."

For a moment he and Jane stared at each other.

"Shall we give him a call?" Jane suggested.

"Why not?"

"This late?"

"He won't mind," Norm said. "Especially if there's some connection."

He picked up the phone and dialed. After several rings, Carl's wife, Beth answered. "Huh…Hel…uh" she mumbled incoherently.

"Hello, Beth?" Norm said.

"Y…uh, Yes?" she said, still more asleep than awake.

"Beth, this is Norm Miles. Listen, I'm sorry to call at this time of the night, but it's kind of important. Is Carl in?"

Beth was now nearly awake. She looked over to her right and saw that Carl was not in bed with her. This was no surprise. "Uh, no," she said, "I think he's at the lab, Norm."

"You sure he went down there today?"

"Yeah…this afternoon, I think."

"Do you have the number?"

"555-6003," Beth said with almost no hesitation.

"Great," Norm said. "I'll try him there. Sorry to bother you." He hung up and immediately dialed.

"Damn," he said. "Busy."

"Try again in a few minutes. In the meantime, here's your coffee. Why don't you restart a fire and I'll be out there in a minute."

"Good idea," Norm said, as he took the steaming mug and headed for the living room.

Once there he turned on the gas, threw in more kindling and logs, and moved toward the recliner. He stopped in front of it. Rather than get *too* comfortable, he decided to sit on the couch instead. It faced mostly toward the fire, but the kitchen doorway that Jane would be stepping through in a few moments was also visible from his spot.

After a sip of coffee, he quickly went back over the day's events in his mind.

They had left Encino at 10:00 a.m. and drove the mile and a half to Carl Maddy's house in Tarzana. Jane had stayed in the car and Norm had gone to the door. Maddy had come out in his robe.

Norm had produced an envelope folded over several times. "Here you go," he'd said. "Salt or no salt? You tell me."

Maddy had immediately opened the envelope and inspected a few fakes. "Well, you're right. It does look like salt...sort of."

"Right," Norm said, "but look close. Remember what I said about the texture? Kind of wrinkly?"

Maddy nodded. "Yeah, it *is* kind of weird looking, isn't it? Did you get it on this trip?"

"Yeah, Grand Cayman."

Maddy looked puzzled. "It's got me stumped," Norm continued, "But Jane is serious. She wants to grow and market the stuff."

Maddy took a sniff. "Does smell damn good," he said.

"You should taste it. Absolutely amazing."

Carl chuckled. "Hell, maybe I'll have a barbecue later. Good on steak?"

"That we haven't tried yet."

After another sniff, Maddy folded the envelope and placed it in his shirt pocket. "Well," he said, "we'll check it out under a scope and see what we come up with."

"No big rush," Norm had said, "but if you get to it this weekend, we'll be at the cabin. You got the number?"

"Yeah, it's in my phone."

"Great. Gotta run." He'd remembered then that Carl had looked up. Dark clouds were rolling in from the northwest.

"Better move it," he'd said. "Storm's due in soon."

"I know," Norm had responded. "We're trying to beat it to the cabin."

With that he'd gotten back in the car, and he and Jane had hit the freeway. They had made only one other stop between there and the cabin, and that was at Willard's, their favorite meat market. Jane had picked up the beef for the evening's stroganoff, several steaks, and assorted groceries for the next few days.

From there, the two had gotten back in the car and driven straight up to the cabin. As Norm thought about this, he had an idea. "Jane," he hollered toward the kitchen.

"Yes?"

"Bring a paper and pencil. I think we'll list out everything we picked up at Willard's. And we'll figure out everything we've eaten off the shelf here, too."

"Good idea."

It had to have been at Willard's, Norm thought. Something they'd bought. The only other possibility was that someone had broken into the cabin in the Miles' absence and laced the pantry items with a hallucinogenic drug, but that seemed next to impossible.

He checked his watch. It had only been a few minutes since he'd tried Carl at the college lab. He decided to wait five more minutes, and then try again. He drew in a deep yawn, rubbed his eyes, and laid his head back.

When he opened his eyes, he gasped.

It was Jane.

She was seated on the couch beside him, smiling.

Norm immediately felt the earlier, sickening feeling flowing into his body.

"Look," she said, in a curt, business-like manner, "we might as well get this out in the open. The truth is, I've been wanting to hurt you for well over a year."

Norm tried to speak but words would not come out. He felt his skin grow clammy. She seemed unaware of his fright.

"Not because I dislike you," she continued, "but because the whole point of this is pain. And we both know that although it may be coming out in the open now, it's been there all along."

She stopped and stared. Her eyes were piercing, brilliant. They took hold of Norm's mind. Her oddly grotesque face twitched downward at the corner of her mouth, waiting for some response from Norm.

Norm could not respond. He was too frightened. He felt like a claustrophobic in a buried casket. He wanted desperately to scream and somehow break free, but he knew it was no use. She had control. And the fear was surrounding him—enclosing him even tighter.

After a pause, she suddenly changed. A kind of genuine excitement came over her. "I can feel what killing—I mean *really* committing murder—would be like," she said. "It's been there all along, Norm, inside my blood, just floating around waiting for a way to surface. I couldn't feel it back then, but now I can feel things better. Everything. So," she finished, now wearing a casual smile, "it's out of the bag!"

"Jane, honey—"

"What a notion," she said, shaking her head with a kind of sentimental fondness. "I do some type of traumatic damage to one of your major organs, and everything just kind of shuts down. All that was Norman Miles seeps out into the cosmos and flickers away into...nothingness! You cease to exist. No heaven. No hell. Just a total and complete end to everything...'Norman'." She looked at him quizzically. "What do you think?"

She had leaned in closer to him as she'd continued to speak. Her face, that horrible representation of his wife, was within inches of his own face. Her pale blue eyes etched their way into his soul. And now she was smiling broadly, loving the fright she could see on his face.

"There's a kind of sweetness and comfort in the idea of nothingness, right Norm? I mean, if we're nothing, we must be everything, right? And..." Suddenly she became sad and bowed her head. "...And this sickness we carry around has nothing to attach itself to. Nowhere to grow and fester and turn rancid in our soul. If we don't exist, the sickness looks for another soul. We're free!" She looked up. Tears came to her eyes. "Norman," she said, "that's what I want for you!"

In the next instant, her huge, cold hand shot upward and slammed into Norm's throat. A deep, frigid pain fired into his neck. He could feel the dry scales on the inside of her palm slicing like small circular blades into his skin. Her nails punctured his jugular.

Blood sprayed out.

Horror flowed in.

Norm lasted only a moment before consciousness was sucked away.

When he woke, she was beside him, a horrified look on her face, gasping, "Norm! Norman! *Talk*, Norman! *Breathe, for God's sake!*"

He gagged, suddenly remembering the huge, constricting hand. He choked and came fully conscious, gasping for air.

Jane held him tightly. "Oh, God, Norm," she wailed. "What now? What was it?!"

In the next few moments, Norm realized it had been another dream. *No!* Not a dream, he suddenly thought, but a *hallucination!* He'd never gone to *sleep!* He'd only closed his eyes for a few seconds!

Jane shook him out of it. "Norm, please talk!"

"I…I'm okay," he managed.

"Can you breathe? You were gagging!"

"Yeah…I'm…I can breathe now."

He was coming back. Jane began to relax slightly. Moments earlier, she had thought sure she was losing him. She'd heard his scream, came running from the kitchen, and found him pressed back into the couch. His eyes had rolled back and his bright red face strained with fear. His mouth was wide open, but he was gagging and choking. Then, just as she'd reached him, he'd just fallen limp. "What in God's name happened?" she said.

"Jesus," Norm said, "I...I can't even explain. You...you tried to kill me."

"Me?"

"Yes. You talked about murder...and—"

"Oh, God," Jane said, "Norm, what's going on? What's *happening* to us?"

Norm laid his head back on the couch and drew a deep breath. He was trembling violently. He had no idea what was happening. "Give me the phone," he said.

Jane picked it up and handed the receiver to Norm.

He listened and hit the hook-switch a few times.

He looked at his wife. "It's dead," he whispered. "Where's my cell?"

Jane found it laying on the coffee table. She flipped it open and saw the glowing message, "Searching for Service". She looked up at Norm and shook her head slowly.

The wind howled in the trees outside.

# Nine

When Kelly and Eric pulled into the strip mall beside The Kingston Inn, the rain continued to fall. Kelly pulled to the side under an overhang. Undecided about whether to go up the mountain, she considering calling her parents again. She tapped the face of her cell phone and got a "No Service" message. "Damn," she said.

"What's wrong, " Eric prodded.

"No cell service. Half the time it doesn't work up here even in good weather let alone a snow storm."

She looked toward the Inn. A payphone hung on a wall beside the office. She turned off the ignition and grabbed her credit card from her purse. She jumped out and dashed for the phone. As she did, she glanced over and saw that Eric's demeanor had not changed. He looked angry and scared.

Arriving at the payphone, she dialed the cabin. It rang, but no one answered. Puzzled, she tired again, this time making sure she was dialing each number correctly. The response was the same. After a moment, she dashed back to the car.

"No answer," she said.

Eric shook his head. "Wonderful. Fucking great! Now what?"

"I don't know…that's weird. They have to be there. Unless they went out or something."

"At midnight in a fucking snow storm? Give me a break, Kel!"

"That's what I mean. They should be there."

"Maybe the rest of the phones are out, too."

Kelly thought about that. It was the logical explanation. The phones at Baldy had a long history of going out in bad weather. In fact, for as long as she could remember the residents' association had an ongoing battle with the telephone company because the lines went out so often.

"So what do you think?" Eric asked, looking nervously out at the darkness and rain.

"We can stay at the Inn. It's right there. But it's only like an hour up to the cabin, and I'd sure like to get out to the lift early tomorrow."

"What about this chain shit?"

"If we go up we'll have to put them on. But it just takes a few minutes."

"I say we stay down here tonight. You got bucks?"

"Yeah," Kelly said, "but I hate to. The Inn is really tacky and I've driven that road a million times. All we'd have to do is put on the chains and go slow."

"What if it's closed up there?"

Kelly pointed across the intersection to a road leading into the darkness. Under a tall pine tree, a large fold-down sign stood locked in the up, or closed, position. "It's not. That's the sign for closures right there. They would have let it down. That's another thing. They may close it yet tonight, so if we're going we need to go now."

Eric fidgeted in his seat. He turned away from Kelly and stared out the window. A moment later he turned back. "Are there like lots of cliffs and shit? Like drop offs?"

Although Kelly knew the road was dangerous in several spots, she played it down. "Not really. It's actually really good road most of the way up. It's just kind of windy at a few places. The whole trick is to just go slow. If you do that it's no problem."

This seemed to make Eric feel a little better. "Fine," he said. "If you want to go up, let's do it. But let's not just fucking sit here."

"What's the *matter* with you?" Kelly finally blurted out. "You've been acting all weird for hours!"

"I'm not acting weird," Eric snapped.

"You are too. One minute you're happy as a clam and the next you're mad and all scared or something."

"Look, Kelly, I'm not mad and I'm not scared, okay?"

"Then what is it? Did I do something? I mean, I thought bringing you here and paying for the whole weekend and everything was…I…I thought I was doing something good!"

"Look, I'm just tired."

Kelly stared at him for a long time. He remained looking away from her out the window. "Are you sure?" she asked.

He seemed to come around a little. "Look, alright, I'm sorry. I mean it. I'm just…I don't know. I just want to get there."

After a long pause Kelly said, "Are you sure you really still want to be with me?"

Fuck, Eric thought to himself. Here it comes. He realized he'd have to play the game a little longer. He had no choice but to kiss Kelly's ass a little, and now she was swooping in for the "Do you really love me?" crisis shit. He turned toward her and forced a gentle look. "Yeah…I really do," he whispered.

"Positive?" Kelly whispered, tears welling up in her eyes.

Eric knew Kelly and he knew the moves. Now even though he was wired and trembling from the waning effects of his cocaine snort at the last bathroom stop, he gathered his composure. He leaned forward, took her in his arms and hugged her tightly. With her head on his shoulder, he whispered. "I'm sorry, Kel. It's me, not you." He followed this with a passionate kiss. After several more kisses and assurances that he loved her, Eric knew Kelly had been "smoothed over".

She started the car and pulled into the well-lit check in area in front of the Kingston Inn. She went inside and asked the manager if she could park the car in their lot long enough to put on the chains. The manager agreed and she and Eric went to work.

Fifteen minutes later, the chains were on. Kelly pulled back over beside the pay phone. The rain was coming down even harder. She checked her cell phone again and got the same "No Service" message. She hopped out and tried the pay phone. Still no answer.

A few minutes later, the Stealth pulled through the intersection and turned onto Mountain Avenue. They came to an almost immediate fork in the road. A large sign stood in its center. Directions for the arrow pointing to the left read, "Mountain Avenue—Pomona". Directions for the right arrow read, "Highway 18—Mountain Resorts".

Kelly made the right and started up the gentle incline at the base of Mount Baldy.

The rain seemed to be letting up slightly.

Eric kept looking around as if straining to see into the darkness.

Kelly was trying not to show it, but she was worried. Worried about Eric and the weather and her parents. But most of all, she was beginning to worry about the drive up the mountain to reach them.

# Ten

Jane rounded the corner and stepped into the dark master bathroom. Before her hand could reach the light switch, she caught a reflection out of the corner of her eye in the large mirror over the sink. It appeared to be a movement of some small shape in the bedroom behind her. She whipped around immediately, stepped from the bathroom, and looked around. She saw nothing but the unmade bed, the end table, and Norm's slippers.

Something was wrong.

She sensed it.

She stepped back into the bathroom, held her breath, and waited. Silence.

The same sickening feeling she'd experienced when she'd sat up on the bed earlier and seen Norm, began to rise again in her stomach. It came slowly like warm, black liquid in a well of horror that she couldn't seem to stop from rising up into her body and mind.

She began to tremble.

"My God, Jane!" she suddenly said to herself out loud. "You're *fine*! You're wide awake and perfectly lucid. No dreams. Nothing. Just calm yourself down, for God sakes, woman! Get control!"

This made her feel better. She took several long, slow, deep breaths. The trembling seemed to subside, as did the nausea. She waited another few seconds, took another deep breath and began to turn back toward the mirror.

In the instant she moved, two things happened almost simultaneously. First, she heard what sounded like a child's anxious voice whispering the word, "Please!" In the next moment, the bathroom mirror again came into view.

A shape. A tiny arm and hand moved into view for just an instant. A child? Impossible! But she had plainly seen the small chubby fingers and smooth white wrist.

Jane gasped and froze. She began trembling uncontrollably. The well of horror was rising. For what seemed like the longest moment of her life, there was no sound or movement. She wanted to scream and run, but the thought of what she might see left her paralyzed with fear and repulsion.

Suddenly a noise came from behind the wall. A tiny squeal followed by a deep, slow whisper, "Here…" A man's voice. Norm's!

It was then that the full realization of what was happening became apparent to Jane. This was not a dream or hallucination. She had walked into the bathroom fully conscious and alert. She'd never even closed her eyes. What she was seeing and hearing at this moment was truly happening! But how on earth?

The whisper came again.

Jane held her breath.

She envisioned Norm—the horrible demon he had become earlier. She imagined that twisted face just behind her next to the wall.

A rustle of sheets and bed movement.

When the tiny hand suddenly came into view again, Jane could stand no more. She wheeled around, dashed toward the door, and looked over her shoulder. What she saw stopped her short.

Norm was naked. He was seated on the floor, legs crossed, with his back against the side of the bed. He was facing the child, a look of sadness on his grotesquely twisted face. The child, a boy perhaps four or five years old, was naked also. He was standing beside Norm, facing him. His body was pale, plump and smooth. He had long blond hair, nearly to his shoulders, and Jane noticed that his tiny right hand was twitching slightly.

Jane's first thought was of paralyzing fear for the boy. What in God's name would the demented thing that was once her husband do to a naked child? And whose child? How had it gotten here? What kind of fright must it be feeling at this moment?

Her concern was short lived. The boy turned and looked up at her. No horror or fright showed on his face at all. His large brown eyes, teary with a kind of odd sadness, looked directly into Jane's. His stare was paralyzing.

With a quivering chin he said, "I…I know, Mom. I know you had to. But…but now what happens to *me*?" The tears suddenly streamed down his cheeks and he started rubbing his eyes, his little hand still quivering.

Norm looked up also. She saw the same look of sadness and betrayal in his face. He was on the verge of crying. "Our son is damaged goods, Jane. He's worthless. Do you have any remorse? Do you realize that you've destroyed two lives…you bitch? You abandoned me and made a perfectly normal little boy into a stupid, fucking, fat little worm?"

She looked at the boy expecting more tears, but he suddenly stopped crying and smiled as if it had all been a joke. He moved closer to Norm, all the while keeping his eyes on Jane. As he placed his arm around the back of Norm's neck and sat down on his thigh, his demeanor changed again. Jane saw deep hatred burning in his eyes. His tiny fingers twitched and he began to rub Norm's ear.

Both he and Norm stared up at Jane. The sensation of utter helplessness and encroaching madness came over her. Their eyes had done it. They were pouring a flood of guilt and horror into her soul.

Jane screamed.

# Eleven

When Gene Aspell finished reading page 349 of the final manuscript entitled *Caribbean Cuisine*, he smiled. It was good. Damn good. Of course this was no surprise to Aspell. After nine years of working with Norm and Jane, and three books, he'd come to expect good. They were both excellent writers with a passion for the best in both food and travel. In addition—and this Aspell knew was their real secret—they had an uncanny knack for approaching the typically bland subjects they wrote about with a perspective that had proven to be fresh, entertaining, and amazingly salable.

Their first book with Aspell, *Tundra Sanctuary*, had sold a hundred and fifty thousand copies, a feat almost unheard of when it came to travel guides. Two years later, *Hot Spots* did even better at two hundred and ten thousand copies. It was a journal-like travel and cuisine book documenting the Miles' travels during one summer in Mexico. *Meat and Potatoes* did nearly as well. An unusual collection of what had always been considered "traditional" Midwestern meals, it also contained interviews with farmers and the housewives who had spent generations mastering the early American recipes that would be sure to leave their men rubbing their bellies and smiling contentedly in an easy chair by the evening fire.

And now, *Caribbean Cuisine*. Lively, spicy, original. This one, Gene thought, just might do three hundred thousand.

Remembering a recent conversation he'd had with Jane from the Miles' hotel on Grand Cayman, Aspell smiled now. He'd been angry that day. The manuscript was late. All their manuscripts were late, and every time they wrote a book, when the original contract date had passed and the manuscript had not shown up, two things had happened.

Marcel Danes, Gene's boss and the publisher at Morton-Carr Press, began to immediately pressure Gene, and Gene, in turn, cranked up the heat on Norm and Jane. This latest book had been no different. It had been two months late, and with their constant travels around the Caymans, Jamaica, and the Bahamas, Norm and Jane had been difficult to contact for much of that time.

Then came the straw that broke the camel's back. Marcel had marched into Aspell's office one morning and dropped the latest copy of a magazine, "Cuisine International", on his desk. It was open to a lead article, which was a review written by none other than Jane and Norm Miles. Marcel was livid.

"We're paying these two damn good money," he'd said, the vein bulging at his collar. "Fifteen percent and full expenses is top dollar. They've got it made. And what the hell are they doing? Running around the Caribbean on *our tab* writing reviews for some Goddamn magazine!"

Gene had been caught totally off guard. He took one look at the magazine and began to boil.

Not more than a half hour later, Jane had called in. "Hi, Gene," she'd said with the usual smile in her voice. "Ready for Washington's Birthday?"

"Washington's Birthday? Why the hell *wouldn't* I be ready for Washington's Birthday?" he snapped. "Nothing happens on Washington's Birthday. But I've got a better question, Jane."

"Which is?" she'd said, the brightness still ringing in her voice.

Referring to the title of the magazine article in front of him, Aspell had said, "Is the Outrigger really sinking? And even if it is, why am I reading about that fact in 'Cuisine International' when a book manuscript you two owe *me* is two months late?"

Jane had laughed. Aspell remembered Norm must have been standing nearby because she'd turned away from the telephone and said, "He read the review." Then as she'd responded to Aspell, the smile had never left her voice. "Relax, Gene."

"Relax? With Marcel dropping this kind of shit on my desk?"

"Look, the Outrigger is a dive and people needed to know that."

"Well, I'm sure anyone who reads the piece will agree whole heartedly. You ripped the place to shreds. But my question remains. What the hell are you two doing writing magazine articles when you owe me a book manuscript?"

"It's going in the mail this afternoon. That's the reason for my call."

At that point, Gene had heard Norm speak from the background. "And tell Marcel he won't be able to keep this one on the shelves."

Gene had responded directly to Jane. "You tell Norm, he'd better be right. The old bastard is having fits."

"Read it and give us a call," Jane had said.

"Where the hell are you two off to now?"

"Home tonight, a week of catch up around the house, then up to the cabin for the holiday."

"Aha," Aspell now understood, "Washington's Birthday."

"Exactly. Kelly's coming down with her newest hunk so we're making a weekend of it."

"Fine," he'd said, "I'll read and call," and they'd both hung up.

The moment he'd placed the receiver down, a word suddenly rang a bell in Aspell's mind. "Washington." Jane had just talked about her holiday, but hadn't he also just *read* that word? He thumbed back through the pages to one of the last recipes in the manuscript, a rare Cayman salad called "Cayman Canellion."

According to what Norm and Jane had written, the two had stumbled onto the chance to try this rare dish by luck. Their write-up spoke of delicious fruits and vegetables grown only in the Caymans, a sweet local oil derived from the seeds of berries known as Limanis, and an incredibly delicious herb or spice of some sort. Toward the end of the piece, Aspell read:

"Up to now, the only name we've been able to discover for this spice is Kassechy. According to our sources that has no real meaning, it's simply a local "handle". But since Washington's Birthday should prove to be a special holiday for us this year, we've decided to name this scrumptious stuff 'Washington's Salt.'"

"Washington's Salt", Aspell thought as he shook his head and again smiled. Jane had come up with the name, he was sure. How she made these connections he had no idea, but they were one of her trademarks. She could mix dog shit with peanut butter, he thought, and find some appealing name for it.

Now he placed the manuscript aside, picked up the phone and called Marcel. "I just wanted to let you know the Miles' manuscript is excellent. We've got a winner on our hands with this one for sure."

# Twelve

"Are you sure?" Sellis asked, coming wide awake immediately. Kaseentilineol Hydrophoxine?

"Not positive," Maddy said, "but it's doing everything according to the article you published in "New Chemist Quarterly" back in '04."

Sellis looked over at his wife. The call had woken her. From her pillow, she whispered, "Is everything okay?"

Sellis nodded to her and gestured that she should go back to sleep. He then turned his attention back to Maddy. "Could you give me just a few seconds while I get to my study?"

"Absolutely. I'm sorry to be calling this late, but it's important."

"No need for apologies," Sellis responded, "I'm always in hopes of receiving word like this. I just need to get to my desk."

"Of course."

Sellis put the call on hold and got quickly out of bed. He took his robe from the hook behind his bedroom door and quickly threw it on. His wife sensed the urgency in his movements. "Something important?" she asked, sitting up in bed.

"A college professor claiming to have some of a substance I haven't been able to lay my hands on in years of research. You go back to sleep. I'll take it in the study."

She turned over and tucked herself in saying, "Don't be too long."

Sellis stepped out of the bedroom, turned on the hall light and made his way down the stairs to his study. There he turned on his desk light, got out a notepad and pencil, and picked up the phone. "So how on earth did you get your hands on it?"

"Two friends of mine," Maddy said. "Just back from the Caribbean."

"Which islands?"

"All of them, I think."

"*All?*"

"Well, I think mostly the Western side. I know they went to the Caymans and Jamaica."

"That sounds right."

"They write food and travel books."

Sellis nodded his head. This sounded right as well. Right, but also extremely dangerous. "So how did they come across it?"

"I'm really not sure," Maddy said. He had no knowledge of a small waterfront restaurant called The Grand Little Cay. Nor was he aware of the events that had taken place there nearly three weeks earlier…

⌘

"Well," Norm had asked, "what do you think?"

"Actually," Jane said, "the escargot is very nice. I like this garlic sauce."

"And the wine finishes well, I think I'd give the squab a B plus."

"Service top-notch…"

"Clean, leafy, tropical motif…"

"And not all that bad on the pocketbook."

"Sounds like we're agreed, then," Norm said. "The Grand Little Cay has found its way into the annals of gourmet history…A toast."

Jane lifted her glass to Norm's and the two toasted.

As their glasses clinked, a tall black man seated nearby in a white suit glanced at the couple and smiled. He then raised his hand gesturing for a passing waiter to bring his check.

"And since I wrote up the White Shell Inn," Jane said, "You get this one."

Norm chuckled and shook his head. "How did I know that was coming?" he said.

He and Jane shared another laugh then went back to eating their dinners. A young waiter's assistant filled their water glasses, as Norm sliced into the second tiny breast on his plate.

Meanwhile, the black man was just receiving his check. "Thank you," he said to the waiter with a heavy British Caribbean accent. "Next time, tell the chef a splash more basil on the squab. Other than that, delicious."

"I'll certainly let him know, sir," the waiter responded.

Norm overheard this comment about the squab. He turned to see the black man giving the waiter a credit card. As the waiter moved off, Norm thought to himself, who ever he was, he had a sensitive and accurate pallet. He was absolutely right. Though Norm hadn't realized it until he'd heard the comment, more basil would definitely have enhanced the taste.

At that moment, the man looked Norm's way. He and Norm shared a glance, and both smiled and nodded briefly. Norm then turned back to his meal and he and Jane continued eating. Several minutes later, he had a thought. "You know what bothers me?" he said.

Jane looked up. "What?" she asked.

"It's all basically the same," Norm replied, as if he had just had a revelation.

"What is?"

"The food. I mean think about it. Here we sit at the end of a three-month stay. We've filled up an entire book with Caribbean dishes, and it's all basically the same stuff with a local twist on it."

As Norm was saying this, the man in the white suit had gotten back his credit card and was signing the receipt. He heard Norm's comment, looked up and smiled again.

Norm continued, "Fish, fowl and hoofen parts. Call it a zillion names, present it standing up, bathed in oil, surrounded by drizzle and mint leaves, but it's all the same— that's what it comes down to."

Jane shrugged. "Well, what do you expect?"

The man in the white suit finished placing his wallet in his coat pocket. He got to his feet, preparing to leave.

"I don't know," Norm answered. "It just seems like there should be something more to this exotic cuisine business. I mean what the hell is exotic about snails and baby pigeon?"

The man in the suit chuckled. "The price tag, of course!" he said in his smooth, charismatic manner.

Norm and Jane both turned. They found him wearing a large cordial smile and just finishing putting his wallet into his pocket. As if embarrassed he'd spoken up, he said, "Oh, I'm so sorry. I didn't mean to interrupt. I'm afraid you just struck nerve."

"You agree, then?" Norm said.

"Wholeheartedly!"

Jane was taken by the man's easy, friendly manner. "So what's the answer?" she asked.

The man shrugged. "I'm not so sure there is an answer," he responded, as if trying to find one as he spoke.

"Except more of the same," Norm filled in.

After a moment, the man came up with what at least sounded like a partial solution. "I'm not sure it's quite that grim," he said. "One always has the option to…well, get off the beaten track."

Jane smiled. "We've been all over Grand Cayman, Little Cayman, Brac, and for that matter, the entire Western Caribbean."

"And we've tried it all," Norm chimed in. "Fish, fowl and hoofen parts—take my word for it."

The man stepped up to their table. "Have you gotten into the smaller villages here on Grand Cayman?" he asked, "The family inns?"

Jane and Norm looked at each other and shrugged. The truth was, they hadn't.

"For instance," the man continued. "There's a very small family run restaurant just up at Venon Loquel. They make a one-of-a-kind salad that…well, exquisite is the word. Terribly unusual and scrumptious. Local fruits and vegetables…It really should be on your list"

"Venon Loquel?" Jane interrupted.

"A small village in the local mountains. Just over to the windward side."

Norm stood up. "Hi. I'm Norman Miles. This is my wife Jane."

The man shook Norm's hand. "Martin Lanteon," he said with a charming smile. "I'm so sorry to have interrupted your dinner."

"No, no," Norm said, "not at all. In fact, I hope you can give us directions to this inn. We're always on the look out for tips from people like yourself."

"We're a book writing team," Jane added.

"My goodness! Writers. Celebrities?"

"Writers, yes," Jane said, "celebrities, hardly."

In spite of the Miles' humbleness, Lanteon became very excited. "Of course I can give you directions," he said. "I know many places here in the Caymans."

"Actually," Norm said, "the salad you just mentioned sounds intriguing."

Jane agreed, nodding.

"Well then the salad it is. May I sit?"

Norm pulled out a chair. "Please do. Can we offer you something? A drink?"

Lanteon took a seat, pulled out a pen and prepared to write on a napkin. "No thank you," he said, "Never touch it. Okay, where are you staying?"

"At the Seabridge," Jane said.

"Fine. You'll want to leave the hotel going east or left if you're facing the ocean...Then you look for a sign a few miles past the Eden Dive Shop..."

The next morning Norm and Jane wheeled their jeep out of the hotel and drove along the shore past homes and small businesses, many half hidden in thick, tropical foliage. A few minutes later, they began winding slowly up the side of a jungle-covered mountain range, enjoying the view as they went. A valley of lush, colorful foliage lay down the side of the entire range and spread like a thick, moist carpet stretching back to the clear turquoise water of the Caribbean.

After a half an hour on the road, Norm had decided that the road was fairly safe, at least in most places. It was an old, potted two-lane highway that mostly wound along the volcanic contour of the small mountains they were ascending. Occasionally it turned inward, however, taking the Miles' into overgrown areas of deep jungle and humid, but refreshing patches of shade.

Had Norm not been comfortable with mountain driving, he might have found the trip difficult or nerve racking. As it was, however, he simply followed the directions he'd been given and maintained a slow speed. He also made sure to give plenty of space to the occasional taxi or car that "flew" past them.

There were frequent turnouts offering a place to pull over, get out, and enjoy the view. The Miles' stopped twice and took several pictures both times. It was just over an hour when they pulled in under a cluster of banana trees beside the bus stop in the center of Venon Loquel. They parked in the shade beside a gold Mercedes Benz.

"My God," Jane said, "strange place for a Mercedes?"

"Maybe this restaurant caters to the very wealthy," Norm joked.

The couple laughed and got out.

The day was extremely hot and humid. At first the only people in sight were a group of three or four adults seated on crates just inside two large, open barn doors across the road. As the Miles' looked around, however, they began to notice more inhabitants. Two small boys were sitting at the base of a huge tree, and a snoozing dog lay beside an obese black woman standing on a porch twenty-five yards to their right. Aside from an occasional brief glance, every-one seemed to be going about his or her business as if the Miles' were invisible.

They found the path noted on their map just to their right under an overhang of leaves and vines. It led away into the deep jungle shade. "Shall we?" Norm said.

Jane smiled. "After you."

The pair started down the path. Eventually they came to a path leading left and an old bridge. They turned, crossed it and moved ahead. Soon they found themselves facing a small red house with a sign out front that read sim-ply "Canellion".

The sign matched what had been noted, but the house hardly looked like an inn. A fifty-year-old two-room shack backed up to a mountain of tropical vegetation was more like it. "What do you think?" Norm asked.

"He calls this an inn?"

"He said off the beaten track. That much was true."

The Miles' had been standing in the sun in front of the small house for several moments when something caught their attention. A small black shape in a white dress had appeared on the right side of the house. It was a young girl standing in what looked like a narrow gravel driveway leading around the side of the house to a backyard. She was staring at Jane and Norm.

The couple approached and found her to be a cute little girl of perhaps twelve or thirteen. "Hello," Jane said.

The girl smiled, bowed politely and said, "Hello."

"We were told that this was an inn…?"

Again the girl smiled. "Yes. Canellion. Only fine Cayman," she said, gesturing inward like a true maitre d'.

"Well, wonderful," Jane said. "That's exactly what we were told."

Norm took out Lanteon's business card. "We were referred by a mister Lanteon."

The girl smiled and bowed. "Yes."

"And he said what you just did—fine food. In fact, he mentioned a special salad you make…" He looked at the business card and another notation Lanteon had written. "The Cayman Canellion?"

Immediately the girl nodded and smiled. "Cayman's Canellion, the finest," she said. "Best in the Caribbean." She then motioned again toward an area behind her and said, "You come right this way, please."

Norm and Jane glanced briefly at each other and followed. The girl led them around behind the house to a quaint terrace. A single, small wicker table sat in the middle of a raised brick patio. A spotless white linen tablecloth had been spread over it and two place settings had been laid out opposite each other. A large glass of water stood at the head of each setting and a white linen napkin lay folded in the face of each plate. The dishes were light blue, very old, and decorated with an intricate white and red filigree pattern. The entire arrangement sat beneath a canopy of ferns, bamboo, and banana trees. At the far side of this little jungle courtyard, a few animal cages were visible. One had doves in it, and the other rabbits.

Rustic, simple, definitely off the beaten track, Jane thought, but also incredibly clean and charming. Though she'd never eaten at such quaint out-of-the-way place, for some reason she felt perfectly safe and at home. "Norm, it's beautiful!" she said.

She could see that Norm, too, was taken by the simplicity and beauty of their surroundings. He was smiling, looking around, and shaking his head in amazement. "Definitely grass roots Caribbean," he said finally.

The girl held out a chair for Jane. She moved forward and took a seat. Norm did likewise, directly across the table from her. The instant they were seated, the girl said, "Thank you," and disappeared around the side of the house.

Jane picked up her knife. It was silver, decorative, obviously very old and worn, but gleaming and spotless. Norm did the same with his place setting. The napkin was pure, spotless white, heavy linen. "You know, for the first time since we've been here," he said, "I finally feel like we're about to have a *real* Caribbean eating experience, not some commercialized copy."

"And everything is so amazingly clean," Jane said now marveling at her glass of water.

"We're going to have to send this Lanteon guy a bottle of wine or something."

"I've got a great idea, Norm! For our next project. *Hidden* spots like this. Anywhere! The Caribbean, Mexico, Europe!"

"We could do a whole series."

"Exactly!"

Just as Norm was about to suggest that the couple pitch Jane's idea to Gene, a smell suddenly drifted out from the house that was as amazing as this beautiful little spot they had found themselves about to eat in.

Jane immediately sat up straight and sniffed the breeze.

Norm cocked his head and did the same.

A moment later, the couple looked at each other. "My God, what is that?" Jane finally whispered.

Norm drew in another whiff. "I have no idea."

"Norm, it's exquisite."

"I haven't the slightest. Some sort of onion?"

Jane sniffed again. "No. Maybe just a hint of something like onion. I have never…"

"A pepper, maybe?"

"No. No, its…"

Suddenly the couple heard a screen door close on the far side of the house, where the little girl had disappeared. They looked in that direction and saw her rounding the corner carrying two large glass bowls on a tray. At first Jane and Norm had the same thought. Whatever was in the bowls was extremely colorful. As the girl moved toward them, the couple could see each bowl was filled with bright reds, yellows, greens, of course, and what even looked like some sort of *blue* fruit or vegetable. In addition to their wonderful appearance, both bowls carried forth the incredible smell Norm and Jane had just noticed.

The girl arrived at the table and placed the bowls down. "Cayman Canellion," she said with a smile, "best in the Caribbean, just for you."

Jane and Norm both looked down.

Some of what they saw was recognizable, but much was not. Crescents of celery, yellow peppers, diagonal slivers of what looked liked the lower ends of scallions, and a wrinkly Romaine type of lettuce were all apparent. But mixed in with them were bright red Kiwi type fruits or vegetables, what looked like diced eggplant chunks, their shiny purple skins intact, and orange, straw-like shoots of some sort. Setting off this colorful mix were tiny, bright blue cubes of something with the lumpy texture of avocado skin. The salads had already been tossed and they were covered in a clear oily dressing with tiny white flakes in it.

Jane was delighted. She hadn't seen or smelled anything so wonderful in years. The connoisseur instinct that had long since been dulled by countless servings of commercial restaurant food had suddenly awakened. Norm was experiencing a similar reawakening when the girl said, "Excuse me, please," turned and again disappeared around the side of the house.

Jane had already spread her napkin on her lap. She lifted her fork and touched a piece of the closest fruit or vegetable with a single tine. As she passed the tine through the oily coating it picked up a few flakes of the white substance. Jane brought it closer to have a look. It was pure white and looked liked salt. Though she had no idea what it was, she was positive of one thing. It was what had been giving off the incredibly wonderful and totally different smell she and Norm had noticed.

Norm had realized the same thing. He had a red chunk of vegetable close to his mouth with a few of the white flakes on it. "Salt?" he said quietly.

"No," Jane said. "I don't think so. Looks like it, but that smell, Norm!"

"Incredible. And totally new. "Well..." and with that he popped the vegetable into his mouth. The taste was exquisite. He closed his eyes, savoring it as he began to chew. Jane followed suit and a few moments later, the couple were enjoying a meal more fresh, cool, and delicious than neither had tasted in longer than they could remember.

After a few minutes, the girl reappeared with a small basket of rolls. Before she could leave, Norm held up a piece of blue vegetable (or fruit, he wasn't sure) with a few flakes of the spice on it. "What is this?" he said pointing with a knife. "Not salt, right?"

"No. Kasseechy"

"Kasseechy? Jane said. "A spice?"

"Yes, Kasseechy. You like?"

"It's absolutely scrumptious," Jane responded.

"Do you grow it?" Norm asked.

At this the girl hesitated. After a quick glance toward the house, she said, "Yes...My Gammy."

Then she turned and left, and Jane and Norm returned to their meal.

By the time both salads were done, Jane had decided that the spice, whatever it was, was the entire basis for the salad's wonderful taste. It seemed to mix with and compliment everything it came in contact with. She had also decided she had to acquire some, and perhaps figure out some way to grow it herself—possibly even find a way to market it.

Norm went along with her line of thinking. "Makes sense," he said. "I mean it's new and original, it tastes great and hell, what can it take to grow the stuff?"

When the little girl returned again, she placed a small piece of paper yellow "sticky-note" paper on the edge of the table cloth. On it was written:

$12.00 Thank You!

This time she stood by wearing a smile. After a moment, Norm realized that she wanted payment for the meal at once. He reached into his wallet and took out a ten, two ones and a twenty.

Jane saw an opportunity and spoke up. "The salads were just delicious," she said.

The girl bowed and smiled.

"My husband and I noticed the…Kasseechy…gives it the flavor."

"Yes."

"Is there a chance we might buy some of it from you? Maybe a plant or two?"

Again, the girl hesitated, but now she seemed more nervous. "No…no plant. My Gammy's."

"Just a bit of the spice?" Norm said, holding up the twenty.

The girl seemed torn. She hesitated, glanced toward the house, and then responded. "Maybe some Kasseechy. I ask my Gammy now." She turned and disappeared quickly around the side of the house. When she returned, she was carrying a tightly wrapped cloth satchel the size of a small egg. "Gammy say okay some Kasseechy." she said with a smile, and exchanged the satchel for Norm's $20.

A short time later, after handing the girl an additional $10, Jane had listed out the salad's other ingredients. Good-byes were next, and Norm and Jane headed back down the path in the direction of their car. The sun had seemed to grow even hotter and more humid in the short time they had spent there. The couple stuck to the shade as much as possible, swatted away the frequent mosquitoes, and eventually made their way back to the Jeep.

The gold Mercedes had not moved. When Norm and Jane drove away, Norm mentioned it again. "Maybe it be-longs to some business tycoon marketing Kasseechy."

He and Jane shared a laugh, then Jane got serious, "Honestly, we have got to find some way to get back here and put our hands on one of the plants."

⚔

Unaware of this entire incident, Maddy continued his conversation with Sellis. "I only know they try food and sometimes recipes wherever they travel.

"Can you tell me about your tests?" Sellis asked.

Maddy referred to his notes and went back over the tests and results in specific detail. When he'd finished, there was a pause at the other end of the line. "What do you think?" he finally asked.

"I think you've got the real thing on your hands. I'd love to meet with you to see for myself and set up more tests. Maybe we could work together on it."

"Absolutely," Maddy said. "I'd love to. The thing is, I have a more immediate problem to deal with. My friends are eating this stuff."

Sellis had known this was coming the moment Maddy had mentioned that Norm and Jane were food critics. He wasn't looking forward to what he had to tell Maddy. "Are you sure?" he asked.

"Norm said they had."

"Did he mention on what foods?"

"No. He just kept going on about how delicious it was and how Jane wanted to grow and market the stuff."

"Did you read my article?" Sellis asked.

"Originally I did. But that was years ago. I scanned it tonight."

"Well, let me tell you what you're dealing with. Kasseentilineol Hydrophoxine is an extremely rare plant substance. We think, and I repeat, *think*, it's a powerful hallucinogen. As far as I've been able to ascertain, it's indigenous only to the island of Grand Cayman and I'll be damned if I could put my hands on any of it—- even after countless interviews and dead-end leads all over that area."

"Why so hard to get?"

"Because its origin and use is religion based—- kept very secretive. An obscure Caribbean religious sect called the Lamsells cultivated the stuff in remote mountain areas during the 1800's."

"For what? Spiritual visions?"

"Actually, no. You'd think, being religious, they'd probably want to use something like that to get in touch with the all mighty, but I'm told that what this stuff does is hardly spiritually uplifting."

"So why use it?"

"To get even with enemies and rid themselves of what they called 'undesirables'—- sect members who wouldn't get with the program—disbelievers, sinners, thieves, traitors. People they considered sacrilegious or a threat to their basic beliefs."

"'Get *rid* of?' What the hell does this stuff *do*?"

"According to Lamsell doctrine, all human beings are born with a single drop of the Devil's blood—a kind of dormant, genetic connection to the underworld, you might say. Because it's such a small amount, their writings held that the Devil couldn't use it as a conduit into any single person's body and soul. Kasseechy, that was the name they used for this stuff, was said to multiply this drop and unleash its supernatural power, therefore freeing internal demons. What that means in scientific terms is that it drove these so called "undesirables" out of their bloody minds—we think due to an onslaught of bizarre, escalating hallucinations."

"Christ!" Maddy said, thinking of Norm and Jane.

"But here's the kicker. Accounts seem to suggest the stuff had two states. In its pure form, straight off the plant, it was harmless. You could eat it all day and be fine. And on other *plant* substances, still no problem. In fact, the Lamsells used it as a spice on many of their fruit and vegetable dishes. It turns dangerous, only when it's chemically *altered* by certain other organic materials."

Maddy thought back to his tests.

Though the substance had been basically oily and unwilling to mix with other chemicals, it had done nothing frightening until the last test—an exposure to animal protein. He remembered how suddenly it had acted exactly the opposite of contacts with other materials, including plant proteins.

The instant it touched the animal cells, it lost its white color, turned to a thin soluble liquid, and was quickly absorbed into the cells. And following this, the cells had begun to change. They'd slowly developed enlarged nuclei, discoloration, and thickened mitochondria. Maddy remembered when he'd first watched the reaction, the word that had immediately come to mind—"deformity."

Animal protein. *"Meat,"* he said out loud.

"That's the theory," Sellis responded. "But only certain kinds of meat. And my belief is that it changes the cells so the flesh becomes a kind of hallucinogenic 'jerky'. Nasty stuff."

Maddy thought back to his brief conversation with Norm on the front porch: *"Good on steaks?"*

*"That, we haven't tried yet."*

"So what did these Lamsells do with it," he asked, "mix it with meat then secretly feed it to their so called undesirables?"

"You got it. And it was always done very skillfully. They'd invite the marked person over for a meal and lace only his portion or slip it into his meat stock without him knowing. They were very skilled at hiding the scent. In some cases they even got family members to betray the victims. They found ways to disguise its smell and color of the white flakes. One way or another, they always got their man—or woman."

"And he or she would slip off into la la land," Maddy stated completing Sellis' thought.

"That's it. Only 'slip' isn't the word. Flail and convulse is more like it. These friends of yours. Can you get to them?"

"I don't know. But what if I'm too late? No antidote or cure for this stuff? Doesn't it wear off?"

"I guess it has to, but most undesirables never lasted that long.

"*Most*? Some made it?"

"I think so."

"How?"

"I don't know for sure. In all the cases I've read about, there were only a few that suggested an undesirable had survived. And of those, I could only find what appeared to be one common factor—temperature."

"What?" Maddy said.

"The Cayman Islands are in a tropical zone. Most times of the year it's warm and humid there, even during the winter months. Sometimes it cools down during the rainy season, but it stays well above the thirties even in the worst storm conditions. According to the record books, though, there have been a few times the weather patterns changed drastically. One year, Brac nearly reached freezing. The data I was able to get my hands on suggests that these few very cold periods coincided with the times a few undesirables made it through a dose of the stuff. I have no idea why, or if the correlation is even valid. It's all my own personal conjecture."

"But you do have record of survivors during these times?"

"Yes."

Again, Maddy thought back to his experiments. When he had subjected the substance to various temperatures, in some cases it become a solid. This would explain why it would lose its absorptive qualities and remain separate from other substances. But that was in its pure state, outside the human body. What about after it had been consumed and assimilated by the protein cells? It would then be absorbed into the blood of any person who ate it and sent straight to the brain. Wouldn't it then be too late?

He thought about Norm and Jane. Had they eaten any of the spice so far this weekend? With meat? "Christ!" he said, his mind racing.

# Thirteen

Martin Lanteon emerged from the kitchen in one of his many trademark white suits and moved out onto the restaurant floor. The area was dimly lit with a tropical, seaside motif. Fishing nets with cork floats decorated the walls and ceilings, conch shell lamps sat on each of the perhaps 25 tables, Large mariner's ropes circled the supporting columns and crisscrossed paddles appeared in various places. Topping off the motif was an abundance of lush island ferns and, palms and a maitre-d's reception station made from an intricately carved ship's figurehead.

Though it was the dinner hour on the island of Grand Cayman, the restaurant was only partially filled. At one table, a group of four, well-dressed locals saw Lanteon moving their way. One of the women in the group called out to him. "Martin!"

Lanteon heard the call, immediately transformed the scowl on his face into a charming smile, and moved up to the group. "Clarion!" he exclaimed, as he bent forward and kissed the woman on the cheek. He followed this with handshakes for the two men, and a kiss for the second woman. "William…Neil…Carla…How's everyone?"

"Wonderful," Marion responded, "and so is the calamari! I just love the sauce."

"I'm delighted to hear that. Actually, it came with our new chef. I think he's going to be a scrumptious addition to an already talented staff."

"Well, if tonight's meal is any indication," William said, "I'm sure you're absolutely right."

Lanteon turned to Neil. "How goes clothing?" he asked.

"Not bad," the man responded. "Tourist counts are up this season and we're getting our share. And you?"

"Excellent," Lanteon said. "I'm up to my knickers in it, actually. In fact," he continued, stepping away from the table, "I'm running behind. I hope you'll forgive me." He turned to leave then had a thought, "Do try the new Yorkshire Pudding," he said cordially, "It's on me." And with that he moved off toward the main reception station. Once his back was to the group, the scowl returned to his face.

When he arrived at the matre-d's station, Samuel Arvel, the restaurant manager, was just stepping up to the station as well. Arvel was a handsome, well built black man of perhaps forty. He wore a tailored black suit and Patten leather shoes. His short hair was neatly trimmed, as was his thin mustache.

Arriving at the station, Lanteon picked up the reservation list clipboard and looked at it. Five names. He slammed it back down and looked to his left. Two busboys were chatting at the doorway to the kitchen.

Lanteon turned to Arvel and snapped, "Get these people working! Now! Or none of us will be here soon!"

Arvel attempted to reason with Lanteon, saying, "Martin, we've just had a bad period. Now that the—"

"Now, I said! I want people busy! And let me make something else clear, Samuel. I've just about had it with all this laziness, and you are not above it all. We either start filling these Goddamned tables, or I start sending anyone—I repeat, *anyone*—I choose off on a long, permanent vacation. Understood?"

Arvel remained silent.

*"Understood, I said?"*

"...Understood."

As Arvel watched, Lanteon stepped away from the station toward the front door.

# Fourteen

When Norm heard Jane scream from the bedroom, he ran in and found her facing away from him. She was sobbing convulsively and staring at the edge of the bed near the nightstand and closet. "Honey, what is it?" He said.

Jane continued to sob, but she didn't turn around. "Jane!" Norm repeated, as he ran to her and stepped around in front of her. "Honey, you—"

What faced him was not his wife.

It was the face of the demon.

And, she had not been sobbing. She'd been chuckling.

In a casual tone she might have used when talking about what a pleasant day it was, she smiled broadly and said, "The thing is, Norm. This is real. We're here for the duration, buster."

Norm stuttered. He started backing away and managed to get out the word, "N…No!"

"Yes!" she chuckled, "Yes, it is! And look what you've gone and done with this poor naked little boy."

Norm fought for logic and reason. It *couldn't* be real. It was impossible. But suddenly a horrific realization awoke in him. He was *conscious*…in his normal frame of mind. He wasn't dozing or spaced or half asleep. He looked around. He was standing in the bedroom of his cabin, totally alert and lucid, but staring into the face of some horrible thing that had replaced his wife. It *was* real! The others had been hallucinations, but this was…or had they? Had they been real, too? Were he and Jane slipping into some bizarre second existence? He was facing her, watching beads of sweat drip down her pockmarked cheeks and forehead, watching the corner of her cracked mouth curl upward with that hideous smile!

He uttered, "God, no!"

When Jane had screamed, the naked demon that had once been her husband placed the small boy aside, stood up and stepped close to her. Attempting to hold back her hysteria, she could only blurt out, "Norm, this is…*real*!"

For just an instant she thought she saw the old Norm. A flicker of hope surfaced. "We thought it was some kind of hallucination, but it's real! We're stuck in this—!"

The face changed back. Whatever part of the old Norm she had seen, or thought she had seen, was gone. The demon was present. It stepped back from her, looked around the room, smiled and said, "God, what an idea!"

Was it real? Was there another Norm? Her old Norm… or…

Then it reached out and took her by the shoulders.

Its hands were ice-cold and hard. It started to speak. Jane twisted, broke free, screamed and ran.

—

Norm was fighting for sanity…for some explanation. Through his fright and repulsion at the thing standing in front of him, he was grasping to hold on to some piece of his Jane, some fragment of the wife he hoped still existed. As difficult as it was, he reached out and took the monster that had been his wife by the shoulders. He said, "Hold on…please. We'll—"

She looked straight into his eyes. Suddenly her face turned red with strain and the veins in her forehead bulged. Norm heard a sudden wet release and smelled something horrible. He looked down. She was urinating on his feet. The foul, bright orange stream of liquid splashed violently. As Norm lunged backward in repulsion, she turned and ran from the room, still streaming urine.

The instant she was gone from his sight, something changed in Norm. He looked around the room. Everything was in its place, right, normal. No urine at his feet. Had it been a hallucination? Jesus! Of course!

He ran to the mirror on the dresser and looked at himself. He was pale, sweating and trembling violently, but otherwise he appeared intact. God! It *had* been another hallucination. And Jane…had she just been here? Her? Or the monster?

He began to panic. Where was she? The real Jane? What had he just done? Was she okay? "Jane!" he hollered and turned and ran from the room after her.

Jane ran down the stairs and an adjoining hallway, and then darted toward the back porch into the mud-room. As she entered, the snow blowing outside was visible through the utility windows. The gusts howled and she could feel the icy temperature radiating through the walls. Reality. She took a deep breath and felt better. She looked around and began to feel as if it had passed. The fright was subsiding, at last, and she began to reason. Was it over? Had it ever *happened*? Where was Norm? What in God's name was happening to them?

It was then that she heard his voice. "Jane, honey where are you?"

The voice was nearly panicked. It sounded real and frightened...normal!

"Here," she screamed, her need to see and hold her husband overriding her fear of what might enter the room. "The porch!"

Footsteps. He was running.

Suddenly the door opened.

Norm had run down the stairs calling to her. At first there had been no response and this had frightened him. Was she herself? Or a grotesque thing hiding in a darkened corner? When he reached the hallway, he heard her call back. It was she! Jane. His Jane! He ran for the porch, rounded the corner and found her.

She *was* normal. His wife was back!

Jane saw her distraught husband standing in front of her. The relief she felt was like nothing she had experienced in her life. "My God, sweetheart!" she gasped running toward him.

He ran forward and threw his arms around her.

They embraced and shivered. "Come on," he said, let's get inside where it's warmer."

They stepped through the door and walked toward the fireplace. A few steps later they were standing in front of the crackling blaze. Both could feel the welcome comforting when Norm stopped and turned to embrace his wife again.

His arms were like two rubbery, slick tentacles. They slithered around her and began to squeeze. He heard a groan and smelled something foul. Her mouth opened and a long, coarse tongue slid out and began to encircle his neck...

# Fifteen

"Look, I appreciate your trouble Doctor Sellis," Maddy said, "but I've got to run."

"Your friends?"

"I've got to call them."

"Well, listen, can we get together soon? I really hope we can work together on this find of yours. It's big, believe me."

"I'll call you tomorrow. We can set up a meet."

"Great. Good luck."

"Thanks."

When he hung up the phone, Martin Sellis was both troubled and excited. The thought of actually discovering and working on Kasseentilineol Hydrophoxine would be a milestone in his career. But remembering the interviews he had done with Cayman Islanders and the secrecy surrounding the drug dampened his exhilaration with a sense of foreboding at what Maddy might be in for.

Turning these two thoughts over in his mind, he made his way back to bed, turned out the light and had a very difficult time getting to sleep.

Maddy wasted no time. He knew the phone number to the Miles' cabin was at his home on his Rolodex. He immediately rushed from the office, turned out all the lights, and ran to the parking lot. He hopped on his Honda motorcycle, turned it over, and sped away. His watch read 9:51 p.m.

The trip home took just under fifteen minutes in normal traffic. On the empty midnight streets of the San Fernando Valley, however, Maddy was often able to cut that time in half. On this night, he made it in six minutes.

He rushed in the door and ran straight to the phone and Rolodex. He dialed. No answer. He tried again and got the same result.

He rushed up the stairs to the bedroom. His wife was sleeping soundly. He woke her. "Sally," he said shaking her gently.

She rolled over mumbling some half sentence.

"Sally."

She woke up, partially.

"I have to make a run up to Baldy. I think Norm and Jane are in trouble."

"Uh…wha—"

Maddy gave up and said, "Sleep tight. I'll be back." He kissed her on the cheek and she was back in dreamland in an instant. He ran to the closet and threw on a sweatshirt, and scarf, a leather jacket, and his heavy leather ski gloves. He darted out the front door, hopped on the Honda, and pulled his helmet down over his face. He kick started the bike and raced away into the shadows. In less than a minute he was on the Ventura freeway headed east. The trip to Baldy was normally around two and a half hours.

# Sixteen

Martin Lanteon stepped out through the front door and left Samuel Arvel furious and dumbfounded at the reception station. Martin felt better. He had at least vented a bit of the anger and frustration that had been gnawing at him for weeks.

The breeze was warm and the sea smelled fresh and salty. Martin looked out into the harbor cove. The lights of two cruise ships, a Carnival and a Royal Caribbean, glittered on the black, crystal clear water of the bay.

Martin knew not only the company that each ship belonged to, but also the name and captain of every ship within the various fleets that docked at Georgetown. The two on the bay at this moment were The Westwind and The Royal Conch II. Their silhouettes, the arrangement of their smoke stacks, and the strings of deck lights told him this at a glance. Lanteon considered the ships, their captains and virtually every other element in his life according to three simple standards: money, power, and possession. And it was because of this perspective that he now felt such anger. His personal reputation had been diminished. He had less money, less power, and less control than he'd had only a short time ago. The passengers in the ships on the harbor were in Georgetown enjoying dinners and entertainment. But they were not at his establishment.

As he stepped away from his restaurant, the neon sign over its front door shown brightly toward the harbor. "The Outrigger: Exquisite Caribbean Cuisine." Lanteon crossed the empty street and got into his gold Mercedes. On the driver's side front seat, his small white terrier lay quietly. When Lanteon got in the dog did not wag its tail or become excited. Nor did it cower or attempt to hide. It simply watched Lanteon enter, sit, and for a long moment look out over the harbor. Moments later, the terrier did not recognize that Lanteon had suddenly had a wonderful idea, and that he was smiling with vengeful satisfaction as he started the car and pulled away from the curb.

At the front door to The Outrigger, Samuel Arvel stepped out and watched the Mercedes drive off.

# Seventeen

Once the Dodge Stealth began the climb up Highway 18 toward Mount Baldy, it took very little time for the rain to begin turning to a freezing slush. Kelly became quiet and focused as she carefully maneuvered the car along the increasingly steep road. She was thankful for the fact that most of the way up the mountain, Route 18 was wide, well-paved, and clearly marked.

Though focusing on the road was her primary order of business, a growing concern for Eric and her parents hovered in her mind as well. The slushy downpour and clattering chains had spooked Eric even more than earlier. These combined with the increasing wind, darkness, and, though she didn't yet realize it, the dwindling effects of cocaine, had moved the boy to a near paranoid state. He was beginning to suspect that the entire trip was Kelly's way of getting even with him because she had known all along he was planning to dump her at first chance.

He thought back to the day she had asked him to go. Was she sincere then or had she been plotting even at that point to draw him into this nightmare? Or maybe it was when she'd come to pick him up and found the girl in his room. Had that been the last straw? The final blow that had made her decide on this torture? But how could she have known? Easily, he decided. She knew the weather forecast. She knew what this mountain was like. She had said herself she'd come here hundreds of times over the years. And knowing those things, she could have simply said, "It's too dangerous. It's not a good weekend. Let's stay here and party instead." Why hadn't she? Why wouldn't anyone with any sense know better than to take him on such a ghastly trip? They would have, he decided. Even her, little miss fat-ass family child wanting to see her parents, would have. Anyone would have. Unless they wanted to get even.

The sudden urge for another snort swept over him. He was coming down. That was part of the problem, he knew. A little lift, even a *small* one, would take him back up and hold him until they reached the cabin. He probably wouldn't sleep much once they'd gotten there, but what else was knew. He hadn't slept more than four hours over the past several days. The coke and drinking binge he and his roommates had been on had kept him awake nearly around the clock.

The Stealth rounded a sharp turn into a steep incline. Kelly slowed, down shifted, and nearly came to a stop. She feathered the clutch, pushed on the accelerator and started up around the turn. The wheels lost traction momentarily. The car jerked sideways.

"Shit!" Eric shouted grasping the dash and mashing his feet into the floorboard.

Kelly held the wheel and hit the brakes. The car came to a complete stop. As she again tried to accelerate, the Stealth lurched backward slightly.

"What the fuck are you trying to do?" Eric screamed.

Kelly gave it more gas. The Stealth moved forward, upward, jerked again, and finally caught. They made the turn. The road leveled out.

Another snort. That was the solution, Eric decided. Jesus. He needed to get off this downer and fast. But how?

Once they were moving comfortably along, Kelly took a deep breath and turned to Eric. "Are you okay?" she asked.

"I'm fine," he said looking out the side window away from her. "I'm just fucking fine."

"I mean, really?"

"Really what?"

"You're acting weird…You're scaring me, Eric!"

"Look, I'm just—"

"You're like panicked! I can see it in your eyes!"

"I am not. I'm just tired."

"Do you want me to turn around and go back down for the night?"

"And how in the hell are you going to do that, Kel?"

"There's a turn-out up ahead. I can hang a U-turn and we'll be back down in fifteen minutes."

Eric didn't answer. He remained staring out into the howling darkness.

"Look, Eric. Like I said, I thought I was doing a good thing, but now I don't know. I mean, I'm really worried about you…and about us!"

Sure, Eric thought. A good thing. A perfect little scheme to get back at me for fucking around. Another snort. God, another fucking snort! The turn out! Of *course*! "Look," he said, his heart suddenly pounding. "I'm just really tired. I've been partying the last few days and I'm just beat. Do me a favor and pull into the turnout. I want to just get some air and take a leak."

Kelly's anger and frustration was changing to concern. She was genuinely worried that he was on the verge of complete panic. A short stop and a little fresh air sounded like a good idea. The rain had turned almost completely to snow, and provided they didn't stay out long, maybe it would help them both get refreshed.

When she pulled into the turnout and stopped, Eric took a deep breath. With the sound of the motor gone, the wind seemed to immediately increase in volume. When he opened the door, the frigid air rushed in. Kelly opened her door as well.

"No," Eric said, "let me just go alone. I want to clear my head."

Kelly's worry intensified. "Eric…" she said, the concern obvious in her voice.

"Look, I'm fine. Just give me a few seconds." And with that he stepped out of the car and moved toward the rear end into the darkness. The moment Eric reached the back bumper he dug deep into his pocket for the small baggy of cocaine. He knew there was a chance Kelly might still get out so he had to hurry. He fumbled with the rubber band and finally got it free. He bent over in an attempt to block the wind as he prepared to dump a small about of the powder in the palm of his hand. He shook the baggy. A small amount dumped out. As he immediately dipped his head into his palm the wind caught it and blew most of it away. "Shit!" He tried again.

As Kelly waited, an irrational fear occurred to her. What if he were so frightened that he wanted out of the car at all costs and would not get back in. No, she told herself. That was absurd. He'd never do something so stupid.

Besides, he seemed afraid of the dark and the weather. But the intensity of his panic kept resurfacing in Kelly's mind. Was he fearful enough to be totally irrational? She struggled with this idea for several moments, and then decided she wasn't about to take any chances.

She reached under her seat and found her flashlight. She opened the door and stepped out into the wind and snow. She thought she heard Eric say, "Fuck!" just as her door was closing. It was pitch black out, but she could make out his hunched over figure at the rear of the car. "Eric?" she called out. He seemed to slip and mumble something in frustration. What the hell was he doing now, she wondered? She stepped toward him, and called out again, "Eric? What are you doing?"

"Christ! Nothing!" came his response, half lost in the wind.

Something was wrong.

She darted around to the rear of the car and pointed the flashlight. As the beam struck Eric, at first she didn't understand. There was something in his hand and he was bent over as if he were coughing or gagging. Nearing panic herself, she stepped closer and started to say, "What's the—"

And then as he turned toward her, she saw fear and frustration twisting his face. It wasn't snow all over his hand. And he wasn't coughing. There was nothing wrong at all. It was cocaine!

"You bastard!" She screamed and ran back for the car. As she opened the door, she realized he wasn't even following. He was too intent on getting his high to even respond to her anger. She dropped back into the car, slammed the door, and started the ignition. She felt his body bump the trunk as he slipped trying to get around to his side door.

She jammed it into first and sped away. In the red glow of her taillights, she could see Eric, his face completely panicked, running after the car.

# Eighteen

Jane looked to her left and suddenly the fireplace appeared very far away. A wave of heat rushed over her. She turned back and for a moment something changed. She wasn't in a room anymore, but rather some huge dark place. Then it was gone—the sense of space and darkness. She was again enclosed, frightened. She looked to her right and Norm was pacing, walking back and forth in…the far distance? Across a dark, grassy area?…Under an archway? He looked nervous and angry. Suddenly he turned.

He took a single step and he was standing in front of her.

At first it really was his face—anxious and concerned. She started to say, "Norm, wha—?" But suddenly, it wasn't Norm, at least not much of him. Once it had been her husband, she knew, but now it bore only the slightest resemblance to him.

Standing above her was a huge, wretched, angry young man—a very fat, hunched over boy, barely out of his teens. He had blotched reddish skin and a foul stench surrounded him. His hair was short and bushy and behind his lips were large yellow teeth. He wore skintight sweatpants, stained and soured, and he was barefoot. He leaned down close to Jane. His round red cheeks jiggled and beads of sweat sparkled on his upper lip. His breath was horrid.

"Look," he said, "I need to explain this to you." After saying this, he started to turn away. Then he thought better of it and thrust his face down close to Jane's once more. "I need you to understand that I'm who and what I am because of you. I mean that. *You.* My world...I mean my entire existence is your responsibility. No matter which side of your brain I inhabit, no matter which world, you own me. You made me—you and that asshole, and you have to take care of me—when I shit, when I puke, when I dig up the fucking dog! Period."

Jane could only tremble violently. She was unable to speak.

Having said this, the boy seemed to feel better. He took two steps away from her and ended up in the far distance at the entrance to a tunnel...no, an overhang, a dark, distant hallway or hole of some kind.

Just when she thought he was going to simply disappear into the darkness, he stopped, appeared to consider another thought, and began to tap his large, bare foot. Suddenly he swung around. He rushed back to her with a single step, now more enraged than before. "Did you hear me, bitch?"

Jane stared, helpless, into the massive grotesque face. The smell was suffocating.

"Well?" he demanded.

When Jane did not respond, he stepped away again into the tunnel. Again he turned around and rushed back. "Okay," he said, "let's do this another way."

He stopped, tapped his foot, and thought through carefully what he was about to say next. Then he swung back down close to Jane. His jowls flapped as his face locked in front of hers. "You need the bruises. I guess I should have known that. You need the deep, ripe yellow ones and the wisdom that comes with them. See, the thing is you need to *feel* what you've done to me, not hear it. You need the misery of my swollen stinking carcass bulging under your skin. Then you'll figure it out. Then and only then will you begin to know how I feel every moment of every day of every year and decade and century and fucking eon. Hear me? Fucking *eon*!"

He turned and rushed away into the distance. Two steps and he was nearly a speck. "Shit!" he said, and the voice seemed to echo in the distance, bouncing off the huge black stone walls surrounding her. He stepped back. "The bottom of the Pacific Ocean is turning to bark. Did you know that? The clouds are full of piss. Right. Just overhead. Let's make no mistake about it Mother dear," he paused and said very slowly, "I can give you…the bruises."

Norm was close. He was a part of this. She knew that, but she wasn't sure how. And now she felt oddly removed from her husband. She was frightened and needed help, but seeing her husband as the source of that help was no longer automatic. Even the worry she had felt for him was becoming more distant. Something inside her was urging her to forget him. A kind of detachment was taking seed in her, and blocking out part of the man and the world she'd longed so much to rejoin. The detachment was getting in the way. She could feel that, but she couldn't do anything to change it, and for some reason, she didn't really want to.

"Now I'm going to be real frank with you," the boy said. "I may be a fatty cake, I may look like a tub o' dog shit and strawberries, but Mom, I deal one hell of a punch."

As he finished this sentence, he held his huge, chubby fist up in front of Jane's face. "The truth is, with this here chunk of fat and bone, I could...I could..." Suddenly he wheeled away, saying, "Awe what the fuck..."

And with that, he spun back, took a huge roundhouse swing and drove his fist straight into Jane's face.

The pain was instantaneous and overwhelming. As the world exploded and she was violently hurled into darkness, she vaguely remembered an image of Norm, leaning in close to her, saying something. Asking her something? What, she had no idea. And frankly, she hurt too much to care...

-=⚔=-

Norm was amazed at first by how far he could see. Above him was a ceiling or sky or something very far off. Very bright...very clear and hot. Jane was seated... against the wall? Near the hallway? And out in all directions were the brown carpets and white walls of this room. Or was it the hot sand and white skies? He wasn't sure, but he was absolutely positive about one thing. The depth of his vision had become seemingly boundless, and he didn't like that at all.

Something about it was wrong.

The heat was wrong, too. And something was missing. Jane was not close by. She was close in some way, he knew, but she was also very far off at the mouth of a hallway. Very far off. That bothered Norm, but he didn't call to her, perhaps because he had other more pressing issues on his mind. Most important, he suddenly realized, was the fact that he was lying down (he thought) and there were hands on him. There were also noises of some kind very close by, but he had no idea what they were. And, God, it was hot! As he thought about all this, in some strange disconnected way, it occurred to him that it wasn't the hands or the heat or the noises that bothered him. It was the fact that he could see forever, but he couldn't see himself or Jane or what was holding him or making the sounds.

And he couldn't make sense of this.

That was exactly what was wrong.

Forever? See *forever.* God! Immense spaces of hot white emptiness. His vision seemed to absorb and crystallize the absence of matter. His eyes could penetrate a pale void as deep as all existence, and even the farthest reaches felt as if they were inches from the surface of his eyes. There were carpets too, and sand. There were also walls and lights and somewhere, Jane was a part of it all, but how he wasn't sure.

The hands. And the noises. They were the problems.

Why couldn't he see them?

And why were they so uncomfortable? So God-damned hot?

This seemed to be happening to Norm for a very long time before another thought suddenly occurred to him. The grip of these hands was not pleasant or passive. He was being held. He was trapped and struggling to free himself! Of course! He had been all along! And when this realization finally did occur, it fired into his brain like a jolt of unbearable fear.

He was lost someplace in the whiteness of forever!

There was no up, no down, no right or left. He was alone.

And it was holding him.

Enclosing him in a vacuum.

Squeezing him.

And though his eyes were as powerful as a gods, he couldn't see the fucking hands! He couldn't see what made the noises! Or where they came from. He couldn't even see himself…his body!

And all this was taking forever…forever…

And Jane was…God!

# Nineteen

Maddy sped along on the wet 210 freeway at eighty miles per hour. He was amazed that in the past forty miles he hadn't seen even a trace of a cop. Earlier he had decided that if he were stopped, which he felt he would be, he would simply explain the kind of life and death emergency he was involved in and ask for their escort. But so far that had not been necessary.

Thankfully the rain was light in Pasadena and Glendale as Maddy continued east. As he raced along, droplets spattering his faceplate, he continually wiped it off as he went over the evening's events time and again in his mind.

Norm and Jane. Had they eaten any of the spice? With meat? The right kind of meat? Which, by the way, was what? And if so, what was happening to them at this moment? Were they hallucinating? Had they realized it was the spice that was causing it?

His phone call to Sellis. Religious origins, ceremonies, undesirables, friggin' insanity. "For God's sake, Norm, how in God's name did you end up putting your hands on the stuff?"

Would they survive? Survivors.

"Sellis said there'd been survivors, man."

But how? Why?

"And what the hell does the temperature have to do with it!—if anything?"

He again visualized the experiments.

If the spice was cold it would become a solid and it wouldn't mix with blood or cells or anything else for that matter. Simple enough. But if it were placed on cooked meat it would no longer be cold. It would mix. And if it were ingested, it would take on the internal temperature of the organism into which it had been assimilated, "98.6 my friends." In either case it would lose its solid, cold state and again become a white "salt". It would be absorbed and…

As he reasoned, Maddy remembered the image of the animal protein under the microscope. The almost immediate deformity that twisted and bloated the tiny cells. "God!" he whispered against the driving wind and rain.

"Cold," he said to himself. "Cold. What the hell is it about the cold!…"

Norm and Jane! They were *surrounded* by cold! Freezing cold. But they were insulated. And exposure to the cold would be the last thing they'd want. Go outside on a night like this? No way. They would turn the heat up…stay by the fire. Stay warm, comfortable…insane.

"Come on, Carl, you old fart. *What the hell does it mean*?" he said as he shivered and sped through the night toward the intersection of the Pomona Freeway.

The rain was thankfully staying light.

The freeway was virtually empty.

"What the fuck is it about cold?"

## Ceremony

An eleven-member council had gathered in a large semi-circle.

Years earlier the jungle had been cleared in an oval shape. Lanterns had been placed on poles to light the area. The sound of insects and night creatures chattered in the darkness.

Inside the oval, the earth had been terraced into a kind of amphitheater, descending three levels to a center hub where a twelfth member stood and a large fire burned in a stone pit. The members wore their traditional robes and sat on the terraces.

As they conversed, some became angry, standing at times and shaking their fist.

In front of each member, two small wooden boxes, each the size of a man's fist, had been placed on ornate metal stands. One was red and the other was white and each one had a decorative, hinged lid. Each white box held two stones—a smooth and a jagged one. Each red box was empty.

The group continued in heated debate for over an hour.

Finally, the leader raised his hands and said. "Shoolean! Que le swillion se jujen."

Hearing this, the others all became quiet.

"Kamoo." the leader continued.

Each person then began reaching into his or her small boxes—first the white one, and next, with a stone hidden in hand, into the red one. When all had completed this, the *leader again gave an order. "Wionlez odo quizal shoo namol. Abooleque."*

*The members each got to their feet.*

*They turned to their right and walked slowly around the oval terraces in single files and down to the pit in the center. As they moved past the position of the leader, each one placed a red box down on a block of granite. Then they moved back up into the oval. Eventually, they had all walked down, placed their boxes and arrived back at their positions.*

*When this had been accomplished, the leader began a prayer. All eleven members of the group bowed their heads and began to sway and chant.*

# Twenty

Kelly slammed on the brakes roughly a hundred yards up the icy road from Eric. The Stealth slid sideways on its chained tires and came to rest beside a large boulder. Gasping with fear and cold, Eric slipped and stumbled toward the car flailing and screaming as he went. The thought of Kelly actually leaving him completely alone on this freezing black stretch of mountain road had sent a bolt of hysteria through him the likes of which he could not have imagined. Approaching the Stealth, he began to gasp out, "Kelly! Jesus, wait! Kelly, please… No! Kelly! *Kelly!*"

When he reached the car, he swung open the passenger side door, and dove inside. He found Kelly leaning forward, her head in her hands. Had she slammed into the steering wheel and been hurt? Been left unable to drive? An instant later, Eric's fear was quelled. She was crying. But she wasn't hurt, she was just mad.

Clutching himself and still gasping, Eric said, "God, Kel, I…look, I just can't explain. But, jeeze…I never wanted to hurt you. That's why I didn't…Look, I swear to God. Hear me, Kel? I swear to God, that's it. I'll never do the stuff again. I mean it! I really mean it…"

He waited, but Kelly did not respond.

Now that he was in the car, and the effects of the huge snort were setting in, he began to feel better—more confident and in control. He reasoned quickly that she was mad as hell, but she wasn't about to leave either of them stranded in a blizzard. It was just a matter of calming her down. Smoothing her off. Playing her fucking game for a while until she decided to come out of her little bitch coma and get them on the road.

"I don't know what it is…I…I just can't seem to get it right. I want to. I mean really. I want to for you—for us, Kelly. I swear to God. I just keep blowing it. I don't blame you for hating my guts."

She stirred. Between weak sobs she said, "*Why*?"

She was giving. That was the first sign, he could tell. The rock was splitting and he was doing just fine. Just fucking dandy, thank you! No Goddamn problemo!

"I…because I'm…I'm not like you. I'm weak or defective or something. That's why I love you. Because you make me see that. You make me understand I've got to be strong and change things in my life."

Kelly turned toward him. "But you *don't*!"

"But I try. I swear I try for you, Kel!"

"You say you do but you don't, really!"

"I don't blame you for being pissed. I…I wouldn't believe me either. I guess I sound like a damn liar, but—"

"But what?" she whimpered.

Ah, yes, folks. There it was. The crack. The opening that would allow "The Man" into her psyche to fix things. "But…I swear on my life, I've never lied to you, Kel. I never *meant* to. When I said I'd stop, I meant it. I really thought I could. I really tried, but God, I just haven't been able to control it. It's like…Jesus, I can't explain it!"

"You need *help*!"

"No. I need you. I swear to God, you're all I need and I can and I will stop using speed. Forever, man. I mean it, Kel."

Kelly sat up and blurted out "And why should I *believe* you? You've been lying to me all along!"

Eric stared directly into her eyes. He paused for a long moment. Finally, very quietly, he said, "I never lied. I love you too much."

Kelly burst out crying and threw herself into his arms. They hugged for several minutes, saying nothing. Finally, Kelly pulled back and wiping the tears from her eyes, asked. "Really, this time? Forever?"

Again Eric's stare was dead serious. "I swear to you on my life."

Kelly smiled. He was back. He was hers and it was okay. She rubbed away the last tears and again threw herself into his arms.

"Hot damn!" He thought. Off to the races—the cabin that is—hopefully quickly, maybe even in time for a little dirty boogie in front of the fireplace!

# Twenty-One

Jane had the urge to lick herself. She began with her palms, stroking first her left then her right with the coarse surface of her tongue. As she continued, it occurred to her that her tongue felt different. She found that if she tried, she could extend it out and not only slide it along her palm, but also encircle her entire hand. As she did this, an odd stretching sensation tingled at the base of her throat. She found that the more she licked, the stretching seemed to intensify, making her entire body tingle.

She was becoming aroused. The sound was part of it. The slippery, liquid lapping that echoed off the cool, dank walls of the cavern she was lying in.

She moved her tongue down to her arm, amazed to find that her it could slip totally around her wrist twice. Testing this newfound skill, she constricted it slightly, then released and pulled it back. It held for a moment, then uncoiled and finally snapped back into her mouth with the fresh, sensual taste of salty flesh on it.

Adding to her arousal was her knowledge that Norm was standing over her naked. Or was he seated high above her on a rock outcropping? She couldn't tell. But she could see that he was watching her movements, and he was framed by a black sky full of stars.

Then she saw the dark, hunched over figures come waddling out from the darkness.

There were six. Like chubby, hairless little dwarfs, they emerged from a wall of undulating shadows and sat on their haunches, watching her intently. They smiled with huge mouths, continually rubbed the sweat from their grotesque faces and talking intently with each other in some gibberish she didn't understand. But that made no difference. They were communicating, she knew very well. They were talking about her, and what they were saying made her skin come alive even more. As she looked them over, she saw beneath their pale, distended bellies the tips of penises between their legs.

It was incredibly hot and she was sweating all over as her tongue found her armpit, slid under and around and began lapping at her spine at the base of her neck. *That sound, she thought. God, that wonderful, exciting sound!*

From above her, Norm called out, "Jane...honey, please!" The intensity in his voice excited her more.

Her tongue found her breast, circled over it tasting the beaded salty flesh, and passed over her nipple. An involuntary shudder passed through her body causing her legs to quiver slightly, and open. As if guided by its own mind, her tongue immediately moved down, slid over the tiny puddle of sweat in her navel, and arrived at her drenched pubic hair. Her hips began to move upward slowly, reaching for the coarse tip. It held momentarily, as if teasing her, holding back what she now wanted very badly. She groaned. It moved down, touched the lips of her vagina and pulled away. She swelled and opened.

Above her Norm got to his feet. "Jane. God, Sweetheart!" he said, beginning to pace along the ledge.

Somewhere, water was dripping into pools and her moaning and breathing resonated off the stone walls. An excitement was surging into her, flowing into her muscles, causing her entire body to writhe with convulsive thrusts.

She heard chattering, looked up and saw the figures—the demons—reappearing out of the shadows. Their penises had grown erect—large, thick and hard, lying on the stone floor between their haunches.

Then, without warning, her tongue shot inside her. Hard, coarse, and deep. Deeper than anything she had ever felt. Hot and painful and reaching, searching her wet, sensitive insides until it found and caressed exactly the right spot.

The orgasm overtook her with a jolt. She screamed as a flood of liquid sprayed from her body and the tongue began to move in and out slowly, lovingly.

The first of the demons approached, lust and excitement sparking in his tiny, red, rapidly blinking eyes. Like the tentacle of an octopus, her tongue immediately moved up and pulled out of her body. It slid back comfortably into her mouth carrying the taste of her wet vagina. "Hurry," she pleaded. "Oh, fuck, just hurry!"

He squatted, placed his huge penis to the lips of her vagina, and pushed forward. "Ahh!" she cried.

Norm was climbing down the rocks, pleading with her as she came again. "Jane! My God, Jane. I'm here, sweetheart!"

The demon's face became frantic with arousal. His now bulging red eyes rolled back into his head as he drooled and groaned. He began to thrust harder, chattering some odd, repetitive sounds as he moved in and out. The others were becoming excited, too. They chattered loudly, spurred onward by the one between her legs.

She came again. Another wave of unthinkable pleasure. Heat. Incredible heat! And then *he* came. God! A fountain inside her. A demonic hose spraying up into her body. Suddenly, he pulled out. She was empty and she hated it. "No! No!" she cried.

Another one stepped forward.

Norm was getting closer, above her. The stars circled in the leaves of tremendous hemlocks that surrounded her. A powerful wind swept over the waves of a black, rolling ocean. Huge roots began erupting from the earth, crawling slowly toward her.

The second demon slid into her slowly, and began. He was bigger, harder than the first.

"Mother! Oh, Jesus, now!"

Then the third one approached. Suddenly he grasped her and rolled her onto her side. He twisted her head and forced his penis into her mouth. And suddenly they were all over her, swarming, pumping, chattering and thrusting like fat grotesque little monsters. And she was gagging, being torn apart with pain and pleasure, her body swelling and bleeding, recoiling then accepting, pulling back then pleading, spraying urine and feces.

Norm arrived.

He reached through the frenzy of bodies grasping for her, but the demons were powerful and enraged with lust, holding on, copulating in a storm of liquid and slithering extremities. And now the pleasure was gone. Shafts of fire surged into Jane's body, searing her insides.

She reached for Norm, screaming for help.

Their hands locked.

"Sweetheart!" he yelled, trying to pull her up but it was no use. The demons were like ravenous carnivores over a kill. And now they were *reaching* inside her! God, trying to crawl into her body cavities like snakes! Her skin began to tear. The bones in her pelvis stretched on their tendons. She felt them begin to break with a series of muffled pops. The pain was unbearable. She attempted to scream but now no sound could leave her body. Norm was frantic, above her. He was trying but couldn't possibly stop the frenzy of the things swarming over and inside her.

Suddenly, two taloned hands grasped her head and jerked it back. Her neck snapped. In the next instant her throat was torn out in a spray of blood and saliva. And as she felt her body ripping, her legs and arms coming apart at the joints, she realized Norm could not save her—ever. This death was just beginning. It would continue, just as it was happening now, forever. The rape and the fire and the swarming would go on beyond infinity.

As Norm fell forward into the frenzy, she screamed a final time, "God, Norm!"

Norm pulled and struggled for everything he was worth, but Jane pulled him closer and closer to the lava flow. (Or was it water?) The heat was blistering his skin as he tried frantically to pull away. It was no use. She was too strong. Out of instinct he screamed, "Jane, honey, please!" but the screams soared out into nothingness on a vast sweltering plain and were lost.

Suddenly, he realized something. He had just *awakened* from a dream! For the briefest time he had passed out from sheer pain and exhaustion and in that moment, he'd dreamt of a different kind of existence. A woman, a peaceful world, a child, tenderness, caring…He had "lived" this dream for what had seemed like years, but in reality it had not been a life, but an instant. A split-second release from his constant misery and fear. And now, as quickly as it had come over him, the dream had vanished. He was back in the reality of hell, fully awake. And he and this horrible being had been doing this same thing—struggling beside the expanses of hell—for eons.

Then Norm realized something else.

Even the tiniest fraction of their struggle had taken forever to unfold. Every word he had screamed had taken years to leave his mouth. There had been nothing before this and there would be nothing after. *Nothing!*

As Jane finally pulled his body into the molten stream, centuries passed. And for Norm, each and every moment was a conscious, measured segment of time. A fractionally, infinitesimally small section of eternity that he was aware of from beginning to end.

As his first area of flesh touched the lava and began to sear and blacken, a thousand years passed. And as his arm sank in, finally the full realization came to him. This process of dying, of being burned alive in molten rock, had virtually no end. And each and every instant would pass through Norm's mind as an eternity in itself. He and this demon wife that had been interlocked forever—in hell.

# Twenty-Two

M artin Lanteon stepped into his home, dropped his briefcase on a whicker chair, and placed the terrier on the Spanish tile floor. Then he turned, and without a word, stomped into the bedroom.

Izella Lanteon immediately saw her husband's rage.

She knew his moods and temperaments like the back of her hand. His third wife, she'd lived with Martin for 2 years. During that time she had come to realize that like most people Martin dealt with, she had been one of his marks. In the beginning he had charmed and impressed her with his charisma and savvy command of the business world. What Martin wanted, he got. Financing, advice, control—and people ready to do his bidding, whatever it might have been. It was those elements that allowed him to open The Outrigger, and what he'd convinced Izella would be the foundation for a massive financial empire.

As first his lover and companion, she'd left a modeling career and family in Spain. In the Caribbean he had made her feel like the princess of royalty, about to inherit the throne of a lush, tropical empire. For them it had been first class or nothing. Their clothes, food, housing, and possessions. All the best. All worthy of a wonderful man so skilled and charming he had what she considered not the slightest chance of failure. Her view of the true Martin Lanteon, the man beneath that charismatic exterior, began to reveal itself only a short time after their wedding.

She often recalled that first incident vividly. They had attended a play and during intermission had struck up a conversation with an Australian banker and his wife. Shortly after they'd begun talking, for some reason Izella had forgotten the name of the man's wife and called her by a different name. An awkward moment had resulted. Izella had apologized for the slip and the woman had accepted gracefully. Martin, however, had not. Izella had immediately seen a change in him. Though he remained charming and talkative on the outside, she noticed a subtext of anger and embarrassment in his demeanor. Several minutes later, he'd suggested that he and Izella grab a breath of fresh air on the balcony before act two. When they were alone, the anger surfaced at once. She remembered the look on his face and his words very clearly.

He leaned down close to her and said, "That man has enormous sums of money, power, and an impeccable financial reputation. I will certainly need his help at some point and up until tonight he has viewed me with great respect. I have worked very hard to establish that relationship. A stupid mistake like forgetting his wife's name could negate that work and destroy the foundation I've laid!"

"Stupid." That was the word she remembered most. He could have said thoughtless, or unfortunate, or even disappointing. But he'd said stupid. As she thought back now on the incident, she realized she *had* been stupid—stupid to take his abuse and simply cower like the dutiful wife without the courage to stand up and demand an apology.

That had been the first time.

From then on, the real Martin Lanteon, the man bursting with arrogance, selfishness and anger, gradually emerged as Izella's husband. He'd first struck her at dinner one night when she admitted she had mistakenly given away one of his fine bottles of wine as a wedding gift. First the rage. That horrible look on his face. Then, without a word, one slap across her face. It knocked her into a corner beside the dining table and he had stormed out. On other occasions he had held her face within inches of the flame on the stovetop, choked her until she'd begged him to stop, and one time even raped her at knifepoint after a furious argument.

Though he could be unpredictable, Izella sensed that on this evening he would remain in control. He had just come in from the restaurant and it was obvious he was angry—but thankfully, not at her.

"Bastards!" he said, stepping into the bedroom. "They think their money is guaranteed, an entitlement. They think it's an endless stream of wealth. A constant flow! And of course they all deserve it whether they do a day's work or not! Bastards!"

He took a deep breath. She thought for a moment he was going to calm down. No such luck. He turned to her. "Does that make you happy?" he asked, his cheeks beginning to tremble.

"What do you mean?" Izella stammered.

"Does some little corner of your mind say 'good for you, you son of a bitch! You deserve it'. Come now, Zell, be honest."

"Of course not!"

"Ah, right. 'Of course not.'" He began to move toward her. Even though I've been a bastard of a husband, you wouldn't do that would you? Your way is loyalty, Zell, *blind* loyalty to be more precise. You're a wife and you have a duty to fulfill no matter how unpleasant the task may be."

He took another step closer to her. "Or is it fear that keeps you in my house?" He became silent, staring at each other. And now she couldn't read him. He had reached a spot right in front of her. "You have the intellect of a door stop, Zell. You and that blind, stupid, undying loyalty of yours." He chuckled, shook his head and continued. "Christ, I should be happy, right? I should be counting my bloody blessings!"

"Well, why *aren't* you?" Izella snapped, then got up the nerve to say. "Look at all we have! The house, the maids, the cooks, the cars…Why can't you be happy, Martin, and just appreciate all this?"

"Why?" he said, leaning to within an inch of her face. Then suddenly he stormed away. A moment later he was rushing back toward her. In his hand was a magazine— "International Cuisine". God, she thought. That damn magazine! Would he ever get over it? He refused to throw it out, and every time he spotted it or even thought about it he flew into a rage.

He stomped up to Izella and smacked it down on the bed. It was open to the review. The large title covered a two-page spread. "Is The Outrigger Sinking?," and just under it was the byline, Norman and Jane Miles. "This is why," he said. "Because of people like these two. People who give not one Goddamned thought…not a bloody iota of consideration to the lives of those they write about."

"Martin, it's been *weeks* now!"

"Right. And business is still horrid!"

"But it won't last."

"And if it does?"

"It won't!"

Without warning, his huge hands shot out and grabbed her by the neck. He drove her backward ramming her head into the wall. Luckily there was not a stud at that point. But the plaster gave way leaving a large indention.

"It will!" He screamed into her face. "Will you quit this always positive always perfect rubbish?" He picked up the magazine and held it up in front of her. "It will because these people wanted to ruin me! But I've had a surprise for them, Zell. They're the ones being ruined. Yes. And what a journey it will be!"

"M-Martin…" she said, dazed by the blow to the back of her head.

"Shut up! Don't say a word! You are too damned ignorant to be a part of this conversation! You hear me! *Ignorant*!"

On that final word, he pulled her out from the wall momentarily then slammed her head back again. It was then that his twisted, enraged face began to fade for Izella. Seconds later, she was lying in the corner unconscious, and Martin was pacing around the dining room, looking at the magazine in his hand.

# Twenty-Three

The snow was blowing almost horizontally into Kelly's windshield. She moved ahead, confident but cautious. She took it very slow and very careful as the Stealth continued up the mountain. And she said little. Though she and Eric had made up, she was still depressed and now questioning her relationship with this boy. Eric, on the other hand, had seemed to have come to terms with his anxieties and found some new well of strength. Ever since the incident below, he had been sitting back in his seat looking relaxed and comfortable. Occasionally he even hummed a bar to two of some song, and tapped his fingers on the center console.

Was it the cocaine? Kelly wasn't sure, but she thought so. She was right. For the remainder of the trip up the mountain Eric felt just fine. He had conned Kelly again. They were finally about to arrive at the cabin and meet "good old Mom and Pop," and unknown to Kelly, he had another stash of coke in his shoes that, if he went light, he knew could last him through the weekend.

Nearly twenty minutes after the incident they were nearing the top. Though not consciously aware of it, Eric's thought patterns were again changing. The last snort was just beginning to wear off. He still felt okay, still in control, but the first inevitable signs of depression and paranoia had begun to creep quietly back into his mind.

The "party" was almost over. At first this didn't bother Eric because he wasn't aware of it. When he did begin to realize it, however, it was still what he considered "no-problemo" because he knew they were close to their destination and they would be out of this horrid storm shortly.

The couple moved slowly around a sharp turn and a sign appeared at a fork in the road. An arrow pointing to the left read: "Lake Gregory Resort 4 miles". The arrow pointing to the right read: "Mt. Baldy—City and Lift 9 miles. The moment Kelly saw the sign she felt better. They were only seven miles from the cabin and most of the rest of the trip was on relatively straight, flat road. They turned left.

"I thought we were going to Baldy," Eric said.

"We are", Kelly said, "but my folks' cabin isn't in Baldy City. It's around behind Lake Gregory."

"Secluded?"

"Like nobody around for two miles. And the deck out back faces forty-seven miles of nothing but pines."

Eric shook his head. Finally! He began to go over the priorities in his mind. Sleep. He knew he had to have sleep. He was approaching thirty-six hours with only a few nods and he needed to catch up. That meant no more coke for the night. He figured with his last hit almost an hour behind him and now wearing off quickly, he'd be able to crash with no problem. To be sure, he'd have a drink or two.

He looked at his watch. Nearly 12:00 a.m. He wondered if Kelly's parents would be waiting up for them. He doubted it, and hoped they'd gone to bed. He knew he'd do much better with them if he could have a few shooters, crawl into a sack, crash for ten or twelve straight hours, and meet them fresh.

Kelly seemed to have read his thoughts. "My parents will probably be asleep," she said. "They'll leave a fire for us and maybe some food out."

"They don't worry about you driving this road?" Eric asked.

"They do tonight because it's so bad out, but usually no. They know I've driven it hundreds of times."

"And they know you'll be totally careful," Eric said with an odd smile.

Kelly wasn't sure if he was serious or teasing her for being a goodie two shoes. "Right," she said, looking for Eric's reaction.

"Just as I expected," he said with the same odd smile.

Then, suddenly, he drew a deep breath, turned white as a sheet, and stared straight ahead out the windshield.

"What's the matter?" Kelly asked, applying her foot lightly to the brake.

Eric didn't answer. But suddenly he began to whine. Still frozen and staring, eyes wide, out the windshield, his chest began to heave rapidly, and with each breath a slight puppy-like whine escaped his lips.

Kelly pulled over. She took him by the shoulders. "Eric!" she said nearly screaming. "Eric! Wake up!"

The heaving and whining continued.

"Eric! Look at me...Here! Here!"

Still there was no response.

For Eric, there was no way to respond. He was only slightly aware that Kelley was holding him and screaming. He was dreaming, or rather, half dreaming. Thirty-six hours without sleep and a constant roller coaster ride of cocaine use had brought him to a point of involuntary subconsciousness. His mind had simply been denied the ability to dream for longer than it could stand. It had begun dreaming on its own, even though Eric was still partially conscious.

For him, it had been an instantaneous transition. He'd said the words, "Just as I expected," and blinked at the same time. When he opened his eyes, he was no longer with Kelly in the Stealth; he was being pulled forward by something he couldn't see. Why he couldn't see it he had no idea, he only knew something was drawing him, pulling him out of his own body into blackness. Surrounding this sensation, someplace in the distance, was Kelly's voice and her hands. They existed close by, but Eric didn't know how or why. He didn't understand the words, because they were in some other world. And the hands. Were they touching him through some warp? He wasn't sure, and it really made very little difference. What mattered was the drawing outward of Eric's soul. The pull toward darkness that was stronger than his will. The terrible, unholy feeling of…

Just as instantaneously as it had come over him, the sensation disappeared. Eric was back. He released the breath and came fully awake. "God," he said, turning to Kelly.

"What happened?"

"Christ!"

"Are you okay?"

"Yeah…I—"

"What?"

Eric knew what it was and he knew why it happened. "I need sleep," he said, "I been up too long."

"What do you mean? Like how long?"

"A few days."

"A few days! Like how many?"

"I don't know. Maybe three."

"Three days without sleep? Eric you're going to kill"—

"Look, I'm okay, let's just head for your folks' place. All I need is some winks."

"Lay back," Kelly suggested. "It'll still be fifteen or twenty minutes. Sleep 'till we get there."

Eric took her advice. He laid his head back and before Kelly had turned the next corner, he was dreaming once again. This time much more pleasantly—of him and the guys snorting coke...

# Twenty-Four

Carl Maddy checked the digital read-out of his watch as he sped along the San Bernardino Freeway toward the Mountain Avenue exit.

12:10 a.m.

Hopefully, Norm and Jane were fast asleep.

Hopefully they hadn't eaten any of the "Salt" on meat, and they'd had a very pleasant and typical evening. A nice fire, some TV, relaxed conversation...and eventually bed time.

Sweet fucking dreams.

And if they *had* eaten the stuff on meat? If it did have them hallucinating? Did they have any idea what was causing it? Did they understand it would pass? If they could just hang on? The fire. Of course they would have a fire, and they'd stay close to it. "What does any normal person do in a mountain cabin in the middle of a snow storm? "Start a fire, my man" he said angrily, "Snuggle up to it. Stay warm... warm, God-damn it!" When all along he knew it was cold they needed. Or was it?

Had Sellis' assumption been right?

Was cold really the antidote? Or was it just a coincidence? For the umpteenth time, Maddy went over it in his head. He went step by step through the tests and tried to find a connection. And for the umpteen time he came to the same conclusion. "Damn it, Sellis, temperature should have nothing to do with it, for Christ's sake, because the stuff will have already been ingested, my friend!"

It would take on normal body temperature and that was that. Whether it got to be 120 outside or 10 below, the inside temperature was constant, or at least very close to constant. So the substance couldn't get lower even if it wanted to! So how the hell could cold have an effect on it? Maybe it couldn't. Maybe it *was* just a coincidence and the temperature had nothing to do with it, which left Maddy back at square one.

Though the rain had nearly stopped, as he moved forward the fine droplets continued to coat his mask and he continually wiped them off.

Up ahead he saw the Mountain Avenue exit sign.

He covered the two miles to the off ramp in a flash and came to a brief stop at the bottom of ramp. Straight ahead of him was a sign. "Mount Baldy Resorts 22 miles".

The arrow pointed left.

He made the turn and raced forward on the wide empty boulevard.

22 miles. Could he make it in 15 minutes?

# Twenty-Five

Her name was no longer Jane Miles. His was no longer Norman.

Neither was any longer a human being. They were beings, yes, but now they had become beings much different than the human kind. Somewhere deep in the recesses of their existence, both knew the change had occurred. Both were aware that there had once been a connection between them, and they had been different at that time. They had been interlocked somehow for some inexplicable reason. Each of their existences had been dependent on the other's and they had occupied some area of time and space totally foreign to their current form.

They also Realized that time had only been a momentary event—one instantaneous burst of light in an otherwise black and empty cosmos. Prior to the event, they had been as they were now. Inside that moment they had become something else, some other kind of dual intertwined entity for only a brief instant. It had been a glorious time, but now that the moment had burned itself out, and they were again what they had always been and would remain for eternity.

But the contents of the event—that moment of light—also remained with them. They knew it had contained something sweeter than the present. They knew it had somehow bonded two beings and involved a period of time which had seemed (at least to those beings) very long, but in reality was only an instant on the cosmic clock.

The moment was over.

The status quo of darkness had resumed.

But there was something different…a change. They we're not static, suspended in the vast oceans of nothingness. They were moving. Slipping toward something, going slowly now but gaining speed. And what they were approaching was some indescribably horrid region of the universe. A place or entity or existence from which they would never escape, and *in* which they would experience the worst horrors of existence.

And there was something else.

They were not alone.

Something was with them, holding them, no, *drawing* them, moving them toward their eternal destination. They knew it was a source of some kind. A power neither could possibly imagine nor escape. And they knew that it hated them with a depth they could never hope to fathom. They knew it hated everything in existence.

And then, again, a wave of hope. A kind of sudden clarity, a remembrance came to them. This journey had begun with the force that had somehow taken them over. A thing that had entered them and begun to feed on their souls. But when had that happened? In what distant moment of time and space? And why? How?

Though Norm and Jane had no real consciousness now, they were somehow both aware of this as a common entity, a common victim, a captor of this immense demonic power. And with this remembrance, a fleeting memory of the spark returned, a fragment of the light they had been a part of. In one instantaneous blinding flash, it told them they were not what they seemed! This was some mistake, some travesty. They were, or had been, something else—something free of the sickening existence they had been swallowed by. They were two things—two entities. Two spirits from a different world, a part of the cosmos that was not a sludge of horror and blackness! They were being deceived...lied to...made to believe they were something else and no hope existed in the universe. But there was hope! Somewhere, somehow, there were boundaries to this thing. This horrible grasp was not absolute.

As this awareness surged into their beings, they felt the tug, the drawing away, from the horror and hopelessness. But following this, like another wave, came the pull inward, away from light. The thing was tightening its hold. It knew they had somehow found a hope of escape! Yes! If they could just hold. Just resist, just find the strength to reverse directions! But the hold was tightening, the descent accelerating. Where was the strength? The footing? The will to turn back?

Just as they had realized a sliver of hope existed, it was wrenched away from them with a violent jolt of acceleration. The thing was angry; it was punishing them for their attempt, for their glimpse of the light. The sickening flood reentered them and their grip was lost. They were moving, slipping into hell.

As the acceleration continued, a new feeling began to come over them. It began with a sensation of weight—a kind of growth or expansion along with their motion. And it contained turmoil of some kind. As if they were writhing and getting larger. In some unconscious way, they felt something was being added to them. Weight. Mass. Size.

Something that was also struggling and pulling, causing their entity to quake and roll in the chaotic darkness. At first they could make no logical sense of what this was or what was causing it. Then, as the process seemed to increase, and, like their descent, gain acceleration, another facet of it began to come clear. It also included a form of sound. Voices. Not one, but many voices. Words, whispers, groans, pleading. Intense sounds. Many, many of them.

And soon they began to understand. They were not only descending by themselves into the fires of eternal horror and misery, they had become a magnet, a sickening maelstrom, drawing, sweeping in other entities as they went. And those entities were struggling for release. Pleading and wailing to be freed. They were souls. Living souls that had been as they had been in the moment of light. Good, caring, loving souls—peacefully intertwined as part of an existence that played out on some distant level of consciousness.

They were friends, relatives, and acquaintances. They were living souls—children, adults, and the elderly. And they were dead souls. And not only were Norm and Jane drawing in myriads of dead and living souls, they were drawing in the stuff of the universe as well. All things. Large, small, good, bad, peaceful, wretched. Electrons, atoms, galaxies, nebula, stars, trees, water, wind—all things that existed in the universe where being drawn with these two souls into eternal hell.

Without voices, without minds to realize or understand what had happened, Norm and Jane wailed, calling out into the universe in a sheer free-fall of horror and hopelessness.

# Twenty-Six

When she finally pulled up in the gravel driveway beside her parents' BMW, Kelly turned off the ignition, drew a deep breath, and relaxed in her seat. Looking to her right, she saw that Eric was still asleep. She considered going inside by herself and letting him sleep for a while, but she decided against it. If he woke while she was gone, she reasoned, he might become disoriented and maybe even panicky. Besides, she thought, he would be in bed in a matter of minutes and they could both get a warm comfortable night's sleep. So, after a few more moments she lightly touched him on the shoulder, saying, "Eric…"

He woke with a start. "God, finally!" he muttered, rubbing his eyes and looking around.

"Come on," Kelly said, "let's get inside so you can get to bed. Can you help me with the bags?"

Still drowsy, Eric mumbled something with the word "fuck" in it as the two got out and moved to the rear of the car. The snowfall had finally stopped and the clouds had broken, revealing a nearly full moon. Under its pale light, the white ground and snow-covered pine trees created a frigid wonderland that brought back memories for Kelly of the many wonderful winter days and nights she had spent at this cabin.

She opened the trunk and she and Eric both lifted out their bags. Eric began shivering. "Jesus," he said, his breath creating clouds in the moonlight, "it's colder than shit out here!"

"Probably about fifteen degrees," Kelly responded. "That's the usual up here on winter nights."

"Let's get the hell inside."

"Go quietly."

The pair moved single file on the snowy walkway. They reached the front door and Kelly slipped her key into the lock. She opened the door quietly and she and Eric entered. Eric closed the door. He and Kelly placed their bags down in the entry. Kelly then led Eric through the kitchen to the large rustic family room. Just as she had suspected, a fire was blazing and there was no sign of her parents.

"My folks are zonked," she said, warming her hands in front of the fire. "Your room is just off the entry. You want to go straight to bed? You probably should."

"Yeah," Eric said, "I need some sleep—bad. Can I get a glass of water?"

"Sure," Kelly said getting to her feet.

They stepped into the kitchen and Kelly opened the refrigerator door. She immediately smelled something scrumptious. Looking down she found a plate under plastic wrap piled with beef stroganoff.

Eric smelled the food as well. "Jesus, what the hell is that?"

"Looks like my mom left us some stroganoff. Want some before you hit the sack?"

Eric took the plate from her and removed the plastic wrap. Under it were noodles and strips of beef in a creamy white sauce. The smell was amazing.

"She must have tried a new recipe," Kelly said. "It smells different."

"It smells incredible."

"Here, I'll nuke some for you."

Eric had already taken a piece of beef in his fingers and placed it in his mouth. "Naw," he said, "cold is fine. You got a fork?"

Kelly took a fork from the silverware drawer and handed it to him. As he stood at the kitchen counter preparing to start stuffing in food, he noticed three items on the counter—a salt and peppershaker and a third clear shaker with a white label taped onto it. On the label were the hand-written words "Washington's Salt". Eric picked it up and smelled it. "Wow" he said, "here's what smells so damn good."

Kelly moved up beside him and looked at the shaker. She also took a sniff. "Right," she said. "I guess my mom used it in the stroganoff."

Eric tipped the shaker and began sprinkling more of the salt on his meal. "Well," he said, "we'll just have to spice things up a little more, here. Damn!" He began to eat.

Kelly scooped some onto a second dish, placed it in the microwave and hit the four-minute button. She then stepped back into the family room and glanced around.

She immediately noticed something odd. A cup of cocoa had been tipped over beside the magazine rack on the far side of the room. Strange that her mother had left it, she thought. As she walked over to pick it up, she noticed that one of the throw rugs behind the couch had been folded half over. Kelly walked over and straightened it. Another odd sign. Her mom didn't leave spills lying around and she was a neat-nick about the carpets and furniture. Kelly looked around the room and saw nothing else out of place. But something was just not…

Just then the microwave oven signaled that her dinner was ready. She walked back into the kitchen, placed the cocoa cup on the counter, and removed the plate from the microwave. She couldn't believe how good it smelled. She was lifting a fork full of beef to her mouth when she stopped and paused.

"What's the matter?" Eric said, finishing off the last of his meal.

"Something's odd," she said, thinking over what she'd just seen in the family room. She placed her dinner plate down on the counter and said, "I'll be right back."

"Can I have a bite?" Eric asked, stabbing a piece of meat on Kelly's plate.

"Sure," she said. Then she left the room and headed for the stairway to the master bedroom. As she walked out, Eric stabbed several more pieces off beef, sprinkled on a healthy dusting of Washington's Salt, and gobbled them down. He then opened the refrigerator and began looking for some beer or wine.

The stairway and the second floor hallway were dark, but Kelly didn't want to turn on a light. She walked lightly to her parents' bedroom door. She stopped and listened for nearly a minute. When she heard nothing, she slowly opened it, stepped in, and turned toward the bed.

The covers had been thrown back, but it was empty. She looked toward the bathroom. Dark. "Mom?…Dad?…" she said.

No answer.

At first she was puzzled, then suddenly a wave of fear began to surface. Where could they possibly be in the middle of a freezing winter night? Their car was in the driveway. There were no neighbors close by. Up until a few minutes ago the storm had been raging. And downstairs, the cup and carpet…

Just then she thought she heard something. A slight thump or movement in the direction of the walk-in closet. She paused and held her breath. It came again. She felt her heartbeat quicken as the fear intensified. She stepped forward. She was about to swing open the closet door when she suddenly heard a voice ring out. "Oh, Jesus!" Eric screamed. "Shit! Kelly!"

# Twenty-Seven

Carl Maddy was thankful the rain had stopped. He had made the turn onto Highway 18 and begun the climb to Mount Baldy. Fifteen more minutes he thought to himself as he cranked the accelerator and sped up. He knew the lower part of the road was wide and well lit, so he reasoned that he could make up valuable time before reaching the windy, upper sections.

Again, the realization of how cold he was led him to the mystery of what it had to do with the power of the substance that Norm and Jane had in their possession. If the temperature of the body regulated the temperature of the drug to 98.6 degrees, he'd already concluded that cold couldn't possibly affect it. "No way," he said out loud. "It's a toasty nine-eight-point-six in there, guys. Ninety-eight-point-six! Got it?"

Then, suddenly he had a thought. What if it wasn't the temperature at all, but a *reaction* to the temperature—-something that happened inside the body as a *result* of external temperature changes? He smiled and nodded. "Ah, now you're getting somewhere, Hoss!" he said, sensing he was onto something. "Out of the box thinking. That's exactly what we need Carl, my man!"

When the human body became cold, the blood vessels constricted and shrank away from the surface areas deeper into the muscles and tissue. This was one protection mechanism the body used to help regulate blood temperature. With the vessels deeper in the tissue, the blood could stay warm easier. Another protective reaction was shivering. Shivering created internal heat. The muscles jerking and quivering warmed the body slightly. And the goose bumps that often accompanied shivering were the body's attempt to raise and thicken the coat of hair humans had once had on them as an insulator against the cold.

Suppose there was something about these bodily reactions that changed the chemical and somehow rendered it powerless. But what? And how? The pressure, he wondered? The pressure created when the blood vessels constricted might change or limit the substance in some ways. And how about in the brain, where the drug took effect? What changed there in cold conditions? The pressure created would be experienced by the entire body, including the brain. "Sure!" he blurted out. "The pressure somehow effects this stuff, guys. And that changes it! Or does it?" There seemed to be no other explanation, but this still didn't provide the final answer.

He continued to explore this train of thought as the wind blasted his facemask and the cold seeped in surrounding him.

If Norm and Jane were relaxing in front of a nice warm fire, they would inadvertently eliminate any chance of experiencing this pressure. "Hell, yes," he said, "that might even magnify the effects! Jesus, could it?"

And if they became frightened, what then? Would they go outside into the cold? "Not on your life," Maddy said. On the contrary they would go the fire—- to the security of light and warmth. "We know that, man. We figured that out already! Tell me something new, idiot."

Jesus! He thought as he cranked the accelerator even harder. The road was wet but wide and empty. And the dangerous turns were still miles ahead of him. He looked down at the speedometer. He was going 84.

# Twenty-Eight

On a day approximately three weeks earlier, Martin Lanteon's wife, Izella, stepped into the Cove Hotel, a small but immaculately clean establishment on the eastern edge of Georgetown. She glanced around briefly, saw that there was no one in the lobby, and moved toward the small registration desk.

From behind the desk, a thin, very old black man in gray Dickey pants and a white shirt looked up and saw Izella approaching. He immediately reached into the key rack behind him and took out the key to room 210. As Izella approached he smiled and held out the key, saying "G'day mum."

"G'day," Izella returned with a smile. "An how's your sister, Lauren, these days?"

The man winced slightly and shook his head. "Not so good."

"I'm so sorry," Izella said. "Has the disease returned?"

The man nodded, his eyes becoming glassy.

"I do hope the best for you both."

The old man nodded appreciatively and now smiled showing several missing front teeth.

Izella reached into her purse and gave the man twenty dollars. "Maybe this can help just a little," she said.

"Yes, mum" the old man replied, as he bowed and kissed her hand. "You're a kind lady."

Izella smiled tenderly. She then moved past the old man toward a narrow wooden stairway. She climbed one flight and turned down a hallway to room 210. She unlocked the door, entered, and closed it, leaving it unlocked.

She immediately moved to the window and opened it. A fresh sea breeze drifted in and several pots of small flowers on the window balcony sent in waves of fresh smells. Through the trees the ocean was visible along with several tile roofs, hillside clusters of palms, and rows of brightly colored homes and fences.

She stood for a time simply enjoying the view and the breeze, and taking in the wonderful smells. Then she slowly unbuttoned and removed her jacket and blouse. Next came her skirt, slip, and nylons. She took a few steps to a full-length mirror on an ornate stand and spent a long moment looking at her brown slender body. For a woman in her forties she was lithe and attractive, the remnants of her modeling days apparent in her graceful movements and posture. She had no visible bruises though several dark marks on her legs and arms remained as reminders of the violations she had endured at the hands of her husband.

Satisfied that she looked attractive enough, she removed her bra and panties and stepped into the bathroom. She took a short, cool shower, and felt wonderfully refreshed when she stepped from the tub, wrapped a towel around her, and moved out of the bathroom.

She looked up to find Samuel Arvel seated in a wicker chair beside the window. He smiled. "Sorry I'm late," he said. "A little touchy getting free today."

"And Martin?"

"He's off to Venon Loquel. I suspect he's decided to even the score for that 'uncomplimentary' review."

Izella shook her head in contempt. "Of course he has."

"He'll be a few hours," Arvel said with a seductive smile.

"Wonderful," Izella replied. "And so our future course of action is agreed?"

"Yes," Arvel responded. "The council met and after some discussions, the vote was unanimous."

"And the date?"

"We think at my the celebration. It should be the perfect time."

Izella smiled. "Of course. We'll celebrate *two* milestones."

Arvel nodded and also smiled. "Both long overdue."

Izella then dropped the towel and stepped forward. Arvel quickly removed his clothes and the couple kissed passionately. They then moved to the bed, still in each other's arms. They kissed gently and lay back, both anticipating a loving and intimate lunch hour.

# Twenty-Nine

Kelly turned and ran for the stairs. She entered the hall-way and rushed down. As she darted across the entry way and into the kitchen she heard Eric again. "Kelly! Fuck!"

She found him standing backed against the island in the middle of the kitchen staring, horrified, and looking into the walk-in pantry. The door to the room had been closed when they arrived, but now it was open fully and as her glance moved from Eric to the direction of his stare, she saw a bare leg on the wooden floor. She rushed forward and was stunned to find her mother, lying splayed on her back, half naked on the floor amongst cans, condiments, and packages of food.

Jane was wearing a robe but it was open and her pa-jama top was pulled up revealing her stomach and breasts. Her bottoms were twisted, torn at the waist, and pulled half off. She had thrown up all over herself. Seeing her mother in this condition was frightening by itself, but Jane was also moaning and whining, her body twitching slightly as if she were in the midst of seizure.

"Oh, God," Kelly screamed. "Mom!"

She got no response. And as she reached Jane's side and knelt beside her mother, she looked into the woman's eyes. She saw a blank horrified stare with no recognition that her daughter was beside her. Kelly quickly pulled her mother's pajamas into place and closed her robe. "Mom!

Mom!" she said shaking Jane. Still, she got no response. "Mom, are you okay?"

Suddenly she saw a momentary spark of recognition in Jane's eyes. Her mother turned slightly toward her and for a brief instant seemed to know her daughter was there. But this was immediately swept away by a look of sheer panic. At the same time a terrible sound rose slowly in the woman's throat. It started as a moan but intensified into a horrified shriek as she began to flail and twist. Before Kelly could do more, her mother had flipped onto her side, brought her legs up and grabbed her knees, locking herself into a fetal position. At the same time she was wrenching and jerking as if her body was in the throws of intense convulsions.

Kelly turned to Eric. He had turned pale and appeared on the verge of panic, as he stood back holding Kelly's partially eaten dish of Stroganoff. "What the fuck?" he said.

"I don't know!" Kelly exclaimed. "God, what's wrong with her?" She turned back to her mother. "Mom! Mom, wake up!" she pleaded, trying to shake and turn her mother over. But Jane was clenched and rigid as if her muscle spasms had locked her joints into an immovable position.

Kelly turned back to Eric. "Call 911," she said! "Hurry!"

Eric dropped the plate on the counter and began to look for the phone.

"Over there!" Kelly said, pointing to the wall phone beside the refrigerator.

Eric ran for it, picked up the receiver and heard silence. "It's dead!"

Just then Jane shrieked again in a voice so piercing Eric threw the phone aside and brought his hands up over his ears. "God, shut her up! Fuck!" he said.

Kelly suddenly wheeled around. Her father! The noise she had heard upstairs in the closet. She got to her feet. "Stay with her!" she said to Eric and darted for the stairs. Eric backed away, a look of revulsion on his face. "Christ, what's wrong with her?"

"I don't know!" Kelly said rushing past her frightened boyfriend.

She bolted up the stairs, ran into the bedroom, and slid open the closet door. "Oh God!" she moaned, again horrified. Norm was huddled in the closet in much the same condition as Jane. He had curled up in the corner, his pajamas rumpled and twisted. He looked up at his daughter and instead of the recognition Kelly hoped to see, a look of terror radiated from his eyes as he groaned and breathed so rapidly it seemed he would hyperventilate any second. Kelly suddenly smelled a foul odor and noticed his pajama bottoms were drenched and stained brown.

"Dad!" She said, "Dad it's' me!" And again she hoped to see recognition, but instead Norm scooted back and huddled farther into the corner. There he began to cry like a small child in the throws of a horrible nightmare.

# Thirty

As Maddy slowed and rounded the first series of dangerous turns, the cold surrounded his face like a painful mask of ice. Wincing from the biting wind, the final puzzle pieces suddenly fell into place. All at once he understood exactly why the cold reversed the effects of the substance.

Prior to this moment, he could not come to terms with the idea that internal temperatures and pressure on the body's network of veins and arteries was the answer. On one hand, it seemed to be the only logical possibility, the only change that he could think of that would take place under cold conditions. But on the other hand, what difference should that make? Pressure might temporarily restrict the flow of the red blood cells carrying the drug, but that wouldn't change things. "And besides," he'd said to himself, "it would still be there, man! It ain't going no where!" So as soon as the cold subsided, he reasoned, the effect would return.

He was about to explore a new line of reasoning when he remembered one of his tests on the substance. When at one point the substance had begun to glow, he had reacted instinctively. He'd quickly dropped the temperature and it had simply vaporized. At the time he'd thought he might have made some sort of mistake and he couldn't understand what had happened. Intent on continuing his series of tests, however, he'd simply gotten a new sample and continued working.

Now he remembered that when the body is exposed to sudden cold and the blood vessels constrict and shrink inward quickly, a series of very slight fluctuations of temperature typically accompanies the constriction. Not simply a raising or lowering, but *both*—a rapid rise and fall of only a fraction of a degree.

That had to be it! As powerful as the molecules were in some ways, in other ways they were very fragile. The slight, sudden fluctuation was all it took. "Of course!" he shouted out loud. "Hell yes, man! It slams 'em! They can't take it! It blows the little bastards apart, right on the spot!"

"Yes," he thought. "Yes, Yes, Yes!" The molecular structure simply broke down and what was left became a different substance altogether—miniscule fragments of waste that the red blood cells would release in their normal circuit through the lungs! "That's it Normy old boy!" he sang out with a proud smile. "Bingo, my man! You got it!"

His thoughts now changed to concern for Norm and Jane in the cabin. What should he do if he found them under the influence of the substance? Get them outside immediately. Of course. No matter how cold it was, they had to be brought away from the fire, removed quickly from the warmth they would naturally gravitate towards. In fact, he thought, probably the colder the better and the quicker the change the better. If his theory was correct, a sudden, sustained drop in temperature—like a blast of frigid air—would shock the body's system into a severe vascular constriction and the accompanying temperature fluctuations would vaporize the molecules instantly.

He was well into the turns and getting close to the cabin. He would be there soon. "Hang on you guys," he said, "Just freakin' hang on!"

# Thirty-One

Unable to move or help her parents in any way, Kelly was beside herself. It finally occurred to her that they had to get an ambulance to the cabin, but she couldn't leave them alone in this condition. She turned to Eric. "We have to get help, Eric."

"Yeah," he said, "no shit, but how?"

"You have to take my car down the mountain and get to the hospital. It's just two more off-ramps off the freeway from where we got off."

"No way, Kelly!" Eric said.

"Eric, you have to!"

"What the fuck! How about you?"

"I can't leave them here like this!"

Eric hesitated, stomping around the kitchen. He knew she was right, but the last thing he wanted was to go back into the freezing night. Then something occurred to him. He could at least get out of the fright and panic of this situation. If he could make it down the mountain, he could get to the hospital and let them take over. It was freezing outside, but the car would still be warm and he could blast the shit out of the heater and take his time. He could also get in a good snort, and lack of sleep or not, that was exactly what he needed right now.

Before he could respond, however, Kelly had seen his fear and she'd gone forward in her mind to plan B. "Okay," she said. "You stay here and I'll go. I know where it is and I know the road. I can get there quicker, anyway."

Now realizing he would be stuck on a black freezing mountaintop with two crazed individuals, Eric knew he had one choice and he had to grab it. "No. No. I'll go. Fuck it."

And it was just as he said these words that an odd feeling came over him. He suddenly felt as if the moment in which he had just said these last words had somehow been stretched and slowed into an unimaginable length of time. If was as if time has somehow warped and he had been stuck for eons in a kind of limbo. And the distance behind Kelly into the closet. It has seemed to become incredibly deep.

Kelly saw the odd look come over him. He paused for an instant and cocked his head to the side as if he had just heard someone say something puzzling.

"Are you okay?"

As Kelly spoke the sensation vanished. "Yeah…Yeah, I'm fine," he said, shaking his head. Everything about this night made Eric want to vacate this house of horrors as quickly as possible. "Give me the keys," he said. "How do I get there?"

"Take the same road back down to the interstate ten freeway. Go left two off-ramps to Euclid and get off to the right. The hospital is a half a block down on your right. Send an ambulance. Hurry!"

Kelly handed him the keys and Eric quickly went for the entry. Just as he arrived at the front door, another wave of bizarre sensations swept over him. As his hand went for the knob he looked down and saw what appeared to be someone else's hand—or some*thing* else's. The hand that turned the knob was coarse and pale. It appeared to be slightly swollen and disfigured.

"Shit," he said as he swung open the door and darted for the car. His head cleared immediately. He was there in an instant and found that Kelly had left it unlocked. He jumped in and turned the ignition key. The engine started and he immediately hit the heater fan notching up to "maximum." The blast of warm air felt wonderful as he slammed the door and belted in. He backed up, swung around, and headed down the road.

"Fuckin' A!" he said out loud. "Freedom from the nightmare!"

He hadn't gotten far when he saw the single light of a motorcycle rider coming up in the opposite direction. "Jesus, buddy," he said. "What the fuck are you doing out on a motorcycle on a night like this?"

As he passed the rider he thought he noticed the man turn toward him and slow down, but Eric had no intention of stopping. He was headed out of this place and he planned to keep on going. Then a thought occurred to him. Could this person provide help? Eric slowed down undecided about whether to stop or keep going.

In his rear-view mirror, he saw the rider stop and lift his arm as if waving to him, but just then something frightful swept over him. For an instant, the person standing beside the motorcycle in the fading darkness was not a human being at all. He, or rather *it*, had become something terrible. A demon—some horrible being trying to con him. Trying to make him turn around and come back so it could feed on him! "Jesus Christ!" he gasped and sped away into the darkness.

# Thirty-Two

M addy knew the Stealth was Kelly's, but as he passed by he saw that a young boy was inside. He stopped and waved to the person, but when the car took off again, he reasoned that his first order of business was to get to the house. He took off again and moments later slid his motorcycle the last ten yards up to the cabin walkway. Lights on. A good sign. He dropped his motorcycle on its side and raced toward the front door. As he was approaching he saw a figure race by a curtained window. "Norm! Jane!" he shouted, arriving at the door and slamming the knocker hard several times.

The door swung open and Kelly stood before him, tears in her eyes, shaking with fear.

"Where are they?" Maddy said rushing in and leaving the door open.

Kelly had no idea what was going on, and she could find no words, but she knew Carl Maddy very well and he seemed to know something about her parents' condition. She was suddenly filled with a flood of hope as she pointed toward the laundry room. Maddy rushed by.

He found Jane just as Kelly had left her—comatose, convulsing and now weeping lightly. He grabbed her under the arms and hollered to Kelly. "We've got to get her outside. Hurry!"

Still baffled, but now feeling sure that Maddy could help, Kelly took her mother's feet and helped the professor slide her toward the front door. Jane began to thrash and howl as if she were being ripped apart at the joints. Maddy seemed oblivious. He continued dragging her saying, "Hurry!" They reached the entry and carried Jane through the door onto the porch.

Moving into the frigid air was like entering a deep freezer. The cold immediately bit into Maddy's hands and face. Rapid breath clouds burst from Jane's groaning mouth as he laid her gently onto her side and pulled her robe open, revealing her pajamas. Then he turned to Kelly. "Where's your dad?" he said.

"Upstairs," Kelly said, her voice jerking with fear and cold.

"Come on. I'll need help!"

"Carl what's"—

"Just come on! Hurry, for Christ's sake," Maddy said racing up the stairs.

They reached Norm and found him in the same state Jane had been in. Working together they drug him down the stairs in the same way they had moved Jane. Maddy took his upper body and Kelly his feet. It took them several minutes and when they reached the porch, Kelly's heart leaped as she saw her mother beginning to come around.

Exhausted, Maddy kneeled on the porch next to them, saying, "Okay now you guys. This has to be it. Come on now...I know this is it, for Christ's sake!"

"What?" Kelly managed to say.

"The cold," Maddy said. "They need the cold."

For Jane it was like resurfacing from some great ocean of horror. She felt the sickness begin to drain from her body and soul. She also felt a lightening of her entire being, a rising up accompanied by a slow release of fright and terror. And somehow it was leading to light. It was leading back; out of hell into a place she knew and loved, a place she wanted to reach with every fiber of her being. She was sensing something else—- bodies, people close to her, people she had to reach, people she loved. God, that idea. Love! It began to take on meaning in her mind once again, like a beacon leading home from a long horrible coma. And finally, out of the depths, her voice returned—and words, words that came from a world she loved, logical human words rising out of her chest to escape her lips, words coming from her own human mouth!

As Maddy looked down on them, Kelly heard her mother say, "My God!" She turned to see Jane looking up at her and Maddy. And Kelly saw recognition in her face. Her mother was still disoriented, still groggy, still horribly frightened, but she was back, slowly coming to her senses. Kelly burst into tears, knelt and embraced her, saying "Mom! You're back!"

And she felt her mother return the hug as Jane whispered, "Kelly!" and also began to cry.

Norm resurfaced in much the same way—- a slow awakening from the paralyzing fear of a comatose horror. In his consciousness, a million scattered fragments of what had once been him began to slowly coalesce, reconstructing themselves in the void like a molecular re-birth. The essence of Normal Miles was being pieced back together, and as each tiny fragment fell into place, the slightest bit of hope retuned with it. It began slowly, just as his descent into horror, but it soon sped up. Hope was coming home. Love was growing in his soul. To him it seemed like a very long time, but it was only a few minutes later that he looked into the eyes of his daughter, his wife, and his good friend and began to cry uncontrollably with a mixture of love and happiness.

Ten minutes later the four kneeled together on the porch, shivering but grateful.

"Let's go inside," Maddy said. "I want to tell you the whole story. But remember something. This is important. I *think* I'm right. If you two start to feel weird, we have to come right back out here."

Norm and Jane nodded and the group went inside.

With the door closed and the fire blazing, warmth returned, as did their true personalities. Just as Maddy had hoped, the symptoms did not return. The cold had done exactly as he had predicted—- shattered the cells that had been poisoning the minds of his two close friends.

"What the hell happened?" Norm asked.

"That stuff you gave me when you two left town?"

"Right," Jane said, "The Washington's Salt."

"Call it whatever you like," Carl said, "but let me tell you, it's some nasty stuff."

As she heard the words Washington Salt, Kelly thought back to her and Eric in the kitchen when they'd first arrived. He'd sprinkled it all over the stroganoff.

"A drug?" Jane said.

"A very rare substance called Kaseentilineol Hydrophoxine. Used by a religious sect in the Caymans to send people they didn't approve of into La-La Land.

"But we'd been eating the stuff for days," Norm said.

"But not on meat, right?"

Norm and Jane quickly thought back. Maddy was right. Until that evening, they had only eaten it on salad, just as they had in the Caymans.

"Until tonight, right? I'll bet a month's pay you had it on meat tonight. Right?"

"The stroganoff!" Kelly said. "Oh my God!" She drew a deep breath. A wave of fear rose in her stomach.

"What's wrong?" Maddy asked.

"Eric! He was starved when we got here. He ate a bunch of the stroganoff you left, Mom. And he sprinkled that stuff on."

"Where is he?" Maddy said, remembering the car he'd passed as he had been approaching the cabin—- the car he was sure had been Kelly's.

"Oh my God, I sent him down the hill to get help! We tried 911 but the phones were out!"

Maddy shook his head and said, "Jesus Christ!" Then he ran for his motorcycle.

# Thirty-Three

It came over Eric with a speed and intensity far greater than Norm and Jane had experienced. The boy's lack of sleep and use of cocaine had brought his consciousness to such a delicate state that the drug tore into his brain and gripped it like the violent, searing hand of the devil himself.

He was rounding a hairpin turn, just thinking to himself how great the heater worked in Kelly's car, when it began. An irrational wave of fear suddenly rose up. He felt terrified for no reason he could explain or understand. He simply looked out at the stands of pine trees covered in snow and glowing in pale moonlight and utter fright and revulsion gripped his senses. He gasped and hit the brakes. He felt his throat constrict, forcing the breath out of his body. For some unknown reason it was as if he were suddenly staring into hell. The trees were fluffed in white. The mounds of snow stretched into the woods in wave-like glowing carpets. On his right, through the few trees on the cliff side of the turn, were stars, darkness and several fluffy clouds backlit by moonlight. To anyone in their right mind it would have been a beautiful scene, but to Eric it some-how represented the end of all sanity.

When he was able to take a breath, his instinctive re-action was to flee. But there was no way he could leave the car and step into this God-forsaken place. He had to get through it. He had no choice. He had to get off this moun-tain and then it would be okay. Then he could sleep and be normal again. He hit the gas, fishtailed slightly, and sped off on a straight stretch of road.

Several seconds later, he thought it was easing up. "God!" he said out loud, thinking now it would be okay. Then something unbelievable happened. The word he had just said, "God," seemed to somehow mix with the hot air blasting from the heater and become something with thickness and texture. He was suddenly surrounded by the sound as if it had substance and was sticking to him, clamping onto his skin like a hot, sickening wetsuit, squeezing his face and neck. Sealing off his mouth and nose. He looked down at his arms and body. He could see nothing on his body, but it was there, suffocating him, and now seeping into his skin and becoming part of him. He screamed out, "Ah! Fuck!" and the same thing happened again. Another wave of sound, this time louder. Another coat of horror, clinging, squeezing.

And then it came on full force.

And as he began to simply scream at the top of his lungs, he became more and more permeated with the waves of terror created by his voice. He could not stop it. The sound was the source of his fright, and each time it swept into him, it caused him to scream again.

And suddenly he was no longer alone in the car. He looked in the rearview mirror to see a large rabid shape rising up in the back seat. It was Kelly, but not the Kelly he knew. She had tiny brilliant green eyes, a swollen forehead, and her mouth was large with huge and sagging lips. A dribble of white foam had run from the corners of her mouth and as she began to slowly smile at him, the lips drew back revealing rotting yellow teeth. "Sweetheart," she whispered in a deep raspy voice, "I know how hard it's been for you. I know the sickness is rotting in your bones. I know, and I love you for that. It's just that I need to see your organs. It's that simple!"

He saw movement in front of him. Large shiny spiders, their bodies the size of golf balls appeared rushing out of the dashboard in waves. They began springing onto his face, biting and stinging. The skin on his arms began cracking and splitting open, spilling out a fatty yellow pussy substance. "Gee," Kelly said, "how much fun is this?"

He opened his mouth to scream and large black beetles flooded out in waves. His body began to peel and split as fountains of urine and feces sprayed the interior of the car.

Moments later he was no longer driving a car on a mountain road, he was slowly disintegrating inside something like a microscopic coffin. He'd been buried alive in a tiny, horrific black space that he knew was lost in the middle of an endless void. And he was trying to move, trying to move his arm up to get room, trying to move his leg a fraction of an inch, trying to turn his head just slightly so he could breath, but it was impossible. He was trapped, held still, horrified, suffocating slowly, being devoured.

And when the realization came that this moment would last forever, that he would never die, never be out of this misery, his mind could stand no more. Suspended in an instant that in his perception told him was lasting an eternity, all connection to sanity and the world around him simply shattered.

Without knowing it, he screamed as his foot slammed down on the gas and Stealth began to gain speed. When it reached the next hairpin turn, it had topped sixty miles per hour, and there was no possible chance to slow or negotiate the turn. But Eric had no knowledge or awareness of what was about to happen. He had come apart mentally in an endless sea of fright and misery beyond any horror he could have imagined. He was no longer Eric Harmon when the Stealth left the road. He was something living, something rotting in a human body, but he was not a human being. And as the sound of the tires on the road was replaced by the windy silence of an object sailing out into the frigid night air, Eric had no idea that he was beginning the arc of a seven second, thirteen hundred foot drop into a rocky gorge called Baldy Hollow.

As frightening as this would have been for him, being fully aware during the seconds before his death was an option Eric would have chosen in an instant. The alternative, which he was now experiencing, was a descent into the most horrific depths of consciousness—taking thousands of lifetimes to complete.

When the Stealth hit the jagged canyon floor, it exploded in a fireball that lit up the entire gorge. Over the next twenty minutes, the crumpled wreckage burned out to an incinerated, tangled mass of steel, bones, and charred flesh.

# Thirty-Four

On the night of Samuel Arvel's ordainment as a Lamsel priest, Martin Lanteon was in an uncharacteristically light and jovial mood. As he opened the door to the Mercedes and watched his wife take a seat, he smiled and quipped, "In you go my lovely lotus."

He then moved around to the driver's side, took a seat, and the couple was off on the twenty-minute ride to Arvel's home at the far end of Plantation Valley. "What a wonderful evening," Martin said to his wife. "Look at the stars. Just beautiful."

Izella Lanteon did not respond. She simply stared out of her window at the calm dark water of the bay across which the lights of Georgetown were visible.

"Are you still angry with me?" Martin finally asked.

"Oh, please." Izella responded, and again became quiet as the couple turned onto Cayman Epiel Highway, the long road that led through dense jungle into the valley.

"These decisions must be made," Martin said after a long silence. "Someone has to place the good of the business first. That restaurant is our livelihood."

"And Samuel has been loyal to you," Izella snapped, "all through the years you and he have worked to make it successful!"

"I agree," Lanteon said. "And for many years he was a valuable resource, a man I could trust to manage the Outrigger as required."

"He is still that man—an excellent manager and a loyal friend," Izella said, her voice rising.

"A friend perhaps, but he is no longer an excellent manager, and with him gone we will return to a course of profit and the respect I deserve."

"How can you say that?" Izella asked. "What has Samuel ever done but give you his sweat and hard work and so many long hours? And now at the blessed time of his ordainment, you dismiss him?"

"As a religious leader he will be perfectly suited, but as a business partner he is incompetent and he must go," Martin declared, now becoming visibly irritated with his wife.

"He is more competent than anyone who has ever worked for you and you know it."

Martin did not answer. He drove on for several minutes, staring straight ahead.

"Why not at least admit it," Izella finally added. "You're not firing him because of his competency; you're firing him because you're afraid of him."

Again Martin offered no response, but he pursed his lips tightly.

A few moments later, Izella continued. "You're afraid that because he has become the favorite of all your employees, you won't get their respect anymore. You're afraid they've all gone to his side now and they're finally ready to rebel, aren't you?"

"I'm afraid of no such thing," Lanteon finally said, in a calm monotone voice.

"Oh, but you are. You're frightened out of your wits."

Martin gripped the wheel tightly.

"Tonight we go visit this man to celebrate his ordainment as a church elder. We eat his food, drink his wine, and pray with our friends. And come Monday you relieve him of his job? And you are not afraid? Come now, Martin. You are petrified that"—

The backhand slap came with stinging force, slamming into Izella breasts. Martin knew better than to hit her in the face. She might bleed or swell up. But her breasts were a different thing. He knew they would ache horribly but no one would ever see the bruising or swelling. Izella screamed in pain one time. Then, with tears of agony welling up in her eyes, she slowly wrapped her arms around her chest, bent forward placing her head on the dashboard, and became quiet.

As the road narrowed and the jungle on both sides became denser, Martin slowed just a bit. He said nothing else to his wife, and he knew she would say nothing else to him for the remainder of the trip. It was nearly nine of clock when the couple pulled into Arvel's long driveway. Theirs was the tenth car to arrive.

Izella had dried her tears and retouched her make up. She stepped from the Mercedes, turned her back on Martin, and started toward the front door. He took her arm and stopped her. "Now you listen to me," he said quietly, leaning in close to his wife's face. "You will not disrespect me with this undignified attitude. You will smile as we go in and you will be the loving, respectful wife our friends expect. Do you understand me?"

His wife remained silent. Martin squeezed her arm tighter and again asked, "Do you understand me, Izella?"

"I understand you," she said staring into her husband's eyes. "Now please let go of me."

Martin released her and the couple moved to the front door. Martin wore a broad confident smile.

The party was lively and enjoyable. All those who came had known each other for many years and they were happy to celebrate the new status recently bestowed on Samuel Arvel. Following cocktails, several toasts and short speeches were given, congratulating Arvel on his dedication, study, and character.

Then came dinner—a buffet style spread, which had been catered by The Outrigger. Assortments of seafood and salads had been prepared along with Lanteon's favorite dish, Caribbean Black Beef—plump ground beef patties with mixed in onions, bell peppers, and mushrooms basted with a spicy Caribbean sauce. When Martin arrived at the table, he noticed that the patties were going fast as were the various salads and fruits. Martin was starved. He and Izella filled their plates and both walked away with generous portions.

As the couple sat down on a bench on the terrace, a few friends approached. One commented on how nicely the food had been prepared and displayed. She also thanked Martin for allowing the restaurant to cater the affair.

"It's really nothing at all," Martin replied. "I'll have to tell the staff on Monday how pleased I was with their handling of the details."

"I agree," the friend said. "They've done a very fine job."

"And the food is exquisite," the friend's wife continued.

"Yes."

"Don't you love the Black Beef?" one asked Izella.

"I adore it," she said. "I'll soon finish mine and possibly a good deal of Martin's."

"I'm afraid you won't have the chance," Martin said with a chuckle, wolfing down the meat in large bites.

Over the next few minutes, several other friends gathered and stopped to chat with the Lanteons. Most thanked Martin for catering the affair and some commented on what a wonderful couple the two made. Finally Samuel showed up and also thanked Martin.

"I felt it was the least I could do, Samuel," Martin said. "I consider you a dear friend and I know what a special night this is for you."

Arvel and Izella traded a brief glance as he responded, "Yes, a very special and important night—not only for me, but the entire congregation." He then turned to the entire group. "And that reminds me, I'd love to show you all the new alter and meditation room I've added. Follow me."

Plates in hand the entire group gathered and followed Arvel out the back door of his home toward a low structure some twenty yards away.

"Have you ever seen such a beautiful night?" one woman commented, looking up at the starry blanket above them.

"Gorgeous," her husband responded.

Arriving at the structure, Arvel opened the door and led the way in. The entire group was just behind him, and

Martin and Izella brought up the rear. Just inside was a stairway leading down to a room below ground level.

The group followed Arvel down.

"A cellar?" Martin asked, starting down the stairs.

"Not exactly," Izella said, and just for a moment it struck Martin odd that she commented as if she was familiar with the room. He was about to ask her if that were the case, when he reached the bottom of the stairs and noticed the door. It was made of a single four-inch thick slab of hardwood and hung on heavy metal bots and decorative hinges. He was so struck by the size and weight of the door that he did not notice the light switch to the room they were about to enter was on the outside.

He stepped into the room at the rear of the group.

It was circular with a dirt floor and a low roof that was barely seven feet from the floor. Its diameter was no more than fifteen feet. As Martin looked around, he chuckled, "My Samuel, what a place!"

"Impressive you think?" Arvel asked.

As Martin stammered searching for the right response, he didn't realize that the group in front of him had begun to thin. One by one people were slowly moving around behind him, still chatting, as they backed toward the stairway. Although he didn't notice this gravitation of guests out of his line of sight, something else did occur to him. For just an instant, as he watched people passing him, he noticed that on each plate were salad, fruit and Black Beef. But, in every case, the people were munching on fruit and salad and the beef was left untouched. This only occurred to Martin as a sad waste and perhaps even foolishness on the part of the guests. The beef was absolutely the best part of the meal;

he couldn't imagine filling up on salad and leaving the patties to become cool and hard. In fact he was just swallowing the last bite of his serving, when the room had cleared. "I don't get it," he finally said to Arvel, who was standing beside him, keeping his attention focused away from the door. "Are you just getting started on it?"

"Actually no," Arvel said. "I've been working on it for months now."

Lanteon was not aware that the group, including Izella, had lined up on the stairs with Izella at the bottom just outside the door.

"But what will you use it for? You'll come down here to pray? Or meditate?" As he said this, Martin looked straight up and saw that there was a single vent pipe perhaps three inches in diameter in the center of the roof.

"Yes, and to give thanks. But not right away. There is more to do first." As he said this, Arvel stepped away from Lanteon toward the door. Lanteon burped, and then chuckled, still facing away from the stairs.

"Well, Samuel," he said, "I have to tell you my friend, in my honest opinion it is hot, suffocating, and genuinely hideous down here. More like a dungeon than a prayer room. I wouldn't be caught dead in a"—-

And suddenly it hit him.

He swung around to see Arvel just reaching the door and turning back to face him. Izella was standing behind him, smiling. He had not seen her looking so happy and gorgeous in longer than he could remember.

He glanced down at his plate. Every morsel of beef had been devoured. The first droplets of sweat fell from his forehead into the empty dish. He looked back up. The door was just closing. He heard the lock clink into place and for a moment it occurred to him that the sound and motion of the door closing had taken a very long time, perhaps a thousand years. "Oh, God," he whispered as the light went out and he was left in total darkness.

*The group of eleven black men and women donned their white robes and assembled in the humid Caribbean night. As the stars arched slowly overhead, they knelt in rows, and began to chant. At the head of the group, the twelfth member, Samuel Arvel, had assumed his new position as its highest priest.*

*Very faintly, the sounds of weeping and pleading could be heard.*

*They would soon turn to scream.*

*The group knew this and they knew the screams would last for many hours. They were prepared for this because of a deep, common conviction that they had just cleansed their sacred order of a terrible, longstanding sickness.*

www.ingramcontent.com/pod-product-compliance
Lightning Source LLC
Chambersburg PA
CBHW050934120626
46552CB00001B/197